Mr. Kafka
and
other tales from
the time of the cult

other books by Bohumil Hrabal

Closely Watched Trains

Dancing Lessons for the Advanced in Age

The Death of Mr. Baltisberger

Harlequins's Millions

I Served the King of England

The Little Town where Time Stood Still

Too Loud a Solitude

MR. KAFKA
and other tales from the time of the cult

Bohumil Hrabal

Translated from the Czech
by Paul Wilson

A NEW DIRECTIONS
PAPERBOOK ORIGINAL

Originally published in 1965 as *Inzerát na dům, ve kterém už nechci bydlet.*

This edition was published with kind assistance of a grant provided
by the Ministry of Culture of the Czech Republic.

First published by New Directions as NDP1315 in 2015
Manufactured in the United States of America
New Directions Books are printed on acid-free paper
Design by Erik Rieselbach

Library of Congress Cataloging-in-Publication Data
Hrabal, Bohumil, 1914–1997.
[Short stories. Selections. English]
Mr. Kafka and other tales from the time of the cult /
by Bohumil Hrabal ; translated from the Czech by Paul Wilson.
pages cm
Translation of Inzerát na dum, ve kterém už nechci bydlet.
ISBN 978-0-8112-2480-2 (alk. paper)
1. Hrabal, Bohumil, 1914–1997–Translations into English.
2. Czechoslovakia–History–Fiction. I. Wilson, Paul R. (Paul Robert),
1941- translator. II. Title. III. Title: Mr. Kafka.
PG5039.18.R2A2 2015
891.8'6354–dc23   2015022094

1 3 5 7 9 10 8 6 4 2

New Directions Books are published for James Laughlin
by New Directions Publishing Corporation
80 Eighth Avenue, New York 10011

A milk shop could sell its wares even in the dark

To begin living for oneself is greater than birth

Disbelief can be understood as indiscriminate attention

In any case, I'm advertising a house I no longer wish to live in.

– Viola Fišerová

Contents

Author's preface   ix

Mr. Kafka   1

Strange People   17

Angel   45

Ingots   55

A Betrayal of Mirrors   77

Breaking Through the Drum   101

Beautiful Poldi   119

Translator's afterword   137

Preface

The stories in this book are an expression of a particular period referred to as "the time of the cult of personality." Anyone seeking to find in this book mere condemnation, a thumbs-down, would be mistaken. During this period, I was living with people who felt, or knew, that every era carries in its womb a child in whom one may not only place one's hopes, but through whom and with whom it would be possible to go on living. They were people who had not forgotten the fundamental house rules of human coexistence and who were heroes if only because they had not succumbed to semantic confusion, but were able to call things and events by their real names and recognize them for what they were.

Thus this book is an expression not only of my own evolution, but of a part of society's evolution as well, a society I live in and that, like me, wishes to live in habitations where humor and the possibility of metaphysical escape reign supreme.

BOHUMIL HRABAL, 1965

Mr. Kafka

Every morning my landlord enters my room on tiptoe. I can hear his footsteps. The room is so long that you could ride a bicycle from the door to my bed. My landlord leans over me, turns, signals to someone in the doorway, and says:

"Mr. Kafka's here."

He prods the air three times with his finger, then walks slowly back to the door, where my landlady hands him a tin tray with a breakfast roll and a small cup of coffee on it. He carries it back to me and because his hands shake, the cup rattles on the tray. Sometimes, after such an awakening, I get to thinking: supposing my landlord came to wake me and announce my presence and I weren't there? He'd be terribly startled, because he's been declaring my presence for several years now, just to remind me of that first week, when they'd bring me breakfast in bed each day and I would be absent.

Back then, the rain was falling as hard as it had in the time of the Flood, the river carried the water along in the same measured tempo as it always had, and I stood in the downpour not knowing if I should tap on the door with my finger or simply walk away. The linden leaves chattered like sparrows in the treetops, the light from the streetlamps oozed through the branches, and in the room beyond the half-open door a body was undressing, for sleep or for love. The light inside the room cast a broken shadow on the white enamel of the door and I wondered if the origin of the shadow was alone or with someone else. I shivered. The night rain was cold and my footprints vanished in the muddy downpour. And yet, I thought, it's good to live in anxiety, good to hear one's teeth chatter in fear, good to push life to the brink of ruin and start afresh next morning. It's also good to part forever and to praise misfortune, like wily old Job. At the time, though, I stood there in the incessant rain not knowing whether to knock on the door or walk away, because I lacked the courage to pluck the eye of jealousy from my mind. I prayed: O Rainy Night, do not leave me standing here, do not abandon me to the mercy of banal beauties; let me at least kneel in the mud and stare at the locked house.

One morning, I asked: "Poldinka, do you still love me?"

"Do you still love *me*?" was her reply.

When next I awake, I'll ask her, "Are you still asleep, Your Holiness?" One day, perhaps, the mirror I hold to her mouth will fail to fog up.

Now I'm walking through Ungelt, gazing up at St. Jacob's Cathedral, where the Emperor Charles was married. Once, on the corner of Malá Štupartská Street, my landlord got beaten up, not for being a detective on the morality squad, but for trying to separate two drunks. There's the little house in Ungelt where I used to have lodgings in the attic, but where a blind accordion player had to go through my room to get to his.

I'd very much like to know how the Emperor Charles loved a princess who could straighten horseshoes and roll metal trays into funnels with her bare hands. Pondering that, I look out at the colonnade where the Marquise della Strada would promenade, and her skin, they say, was so silken that when she drank red wine it was as if she'd poured the wine into a glass flute.

I enter the building where I live. In the old days, a bell in the Tyn Church's spire broke loose mid-peal, plummeted through the air, through the tiled roof, through the ceiling, and into the room I now occupy. Now, the landlady is leaning against the window frame lost in thought; the curtains billow and the invisible world is refreshed. Leaning out of my third-floor window I can almost touch the church's stone wall. My landlady lets her russet hair tumble over me like asparagus fronds. Her breath smells of blueberry wine. I gaze at the Mother of God affixed to the church wall, looking as grave as the Margrave Gero. Pedestrians stroll past the bomb-damaged town hall and greet the unknown soldier.

"You know what?" my landlady whispers at my back. "How would it be if we just gave each other a friendly little kiss. How about it, Mr. Kafka?"

"I'm sorry, ma'am," I say, "but I'm true to my girl."

"Look at you!" she hisses. "But you're hot stuff when it comes to boozing and lollygagging around." And she sweeps out of the room, leaving behind the lingering aroma of blueberry wine. The curtains billow, subside, then a thousand hummingbirds lift the organdy fabric in their tiny beaks like the train of a royal wedding gown, and the curtains billow again in the breeze. Somewhere in the building, someone is playing piano exercises from Czerny's *School of Velocity*; a shabbily dressed man stands below the window, his face as pockmarked as his vulcanite suitcase. Mercury runs down the church wall. Bloated owls and baboons have fallen asleep on the cornices.

"May I interest you in these toothbrushes?"

"No, that's impossible."

"All the way from France, and of course, yes, they're nylon – two hundred and sixty-eight crowns a dozen."

"No, no, no – that's impossible!"

"Too expensive? Maybe so, but imagine, sir, how elegantly your customers will swirl round the dance floor polished with our product."

"So that's why she made such a fuss."

"And for something new, I can tell you that we have children's hairbrushes in stock. Can I put you down for some?"

"Yes, but I can never bring myself to leave her."

"Indeed, and the raw material is a hard-currency item."

"I'll drown your house in flowers and curses."

"And I'll give you two percent off if you pay in cash."

"I could send the goods *franco à bord* and you'd have them next week. What's this? It's a concoction made by Hřivnáč & Co. Yes, the one who hung himself. Why? I couldn't say. You'd have to tell me first why our district judge went mad and why the coroner laughed. Just tighten your tie a little and ask your shadow: brother, are you really living?"

I leap out of bed, crane my neck out the window, and look into the street as if peering down a well. I see a blonde female head nestling up to a young man, hear the sound of kisses like the crack of a whip carried all the way to my bedside by the breeze.

4

"Don't back away. You can't have gone off me completely," the blonde implores, and bubbles of silence rise to the moon chinning itself on the crossbar of the night. I can still hear the cook that used to live here snoring through three walls. He snored so loudly I had to buy a fresh loaf of bread every day and plug my ears with soft tampons of bread, walling myself in each night, just so I could get to sleep. Now the blonde lies back tenderly on a pile of sand beside the church and pulls the young man down on top of her, setting loose several plaster-covered metal hoops that clatter over the lovers, but they're oblivious. A white hoop rolls down the narrow alley like a full moon. The Mother of God's hands are locked in cement and she can't even shield her son's eyes.

The Figaro Bar, the Spider, the Chapeau Rouge, the Romania, and the Magnet are all closing for the night. Someone around the corner vomits, and near the Old Town Square a citizen yells: "I, sir, am a proud Czechoslovak!"

Someone else slaps his face and says, "So what?"

A woman with blood streaming from her nose looks out from under a colonnade as though she, too, had just told the same mean-spirited citizen that she was a proud Czechoslovak. And in the middle of the square, a man in black drags a woman wearing a floral dress through a puddle, cursing the heavens. "A right slut I married!"

The woman clings to his legs but the man in black kicks her away. Curling up, she collapses in the pool of water, a photograph in an oval frame, her hair floating like seaweed in the filthy water. Finally the man is satisfied. He kneels in the water, twists her hair into a wet knot, turns her weeping face upward, and runs a loving finger over her features. Then he helps her to her feet, they cling to each other, kiss, and together they walk slowly away, like the holy family. When they reach the Small Square, just outside the Prince Regent, the man in black flings his arms wide as if unsheathing a sword from its scabbard and declares to the empty square: "The spirit has triumphed over the flesh!"

A streetcar rumbles by with a few dead men inside hanging by their hands. A pedestrian stumbles to his knees and tries to ignite a cobblestone. A giant bull bestrides the city, invisible except for a set of pink testicles.

Sometime before noon, I'm walking to the open-air market U Kotců. On the corner, I buy a horoscope for every month of the year and watch colored ribbons streaming from the salesgirls' noses as they measure the material with their arms. Each day, sun umbrellas sprout from the heads of the crones selling medicinal herbs. I often see old ladies tottering out of the dark recesses of the market, their faces scarred with signs of the zodiac, two patches of leopard spots for eyes, dragging their outlandish knickknacks into the light of day. One of them is selling green roses made from tiny feathers, an admiral's sword, and accordion buttons, another is offering war-surplus boxer shorts, canvas waterbuckets, and a stuffed monkey. In the Coal Market, the salesgirls carry tulips of every color around in their kangaroo pouches. Doves bill and coo in the shop windows on Rytířská Street, and parakeets flit about in their cages like poetic metaphors. Several Canadian hamsters are working their way to freedom in the tall chimneys of their glass cages. Once, for three hundred crowns, I became a saint for an instant: I bought up all the goldfinches, then released them from my hand. Oh, what a feeling when a terrified little bird flies from your palm to freedom!

I enter the covered market where old ladies sell blood pudding by the plateful. The air in here smells of newborn babies, damp garlic clusters, vinegar, and hemp. Men are unloading slaughtered lambs from the backs of trucks. Strange how the high holidays demand animal sacrifice: fish at Christmas; goats and lambs at Easter. I think of the time we slaughtered a pig back home and bungled slitting its throat and it burrowed into the manure pile, preferring to drown in piss and shit rather than face once more the butcher with a knife in his hands.

I get a move on, but it's too late. The bucket of beer I'd gone out to fetch has gone flat. In the office of the Zinner Brothers, with its five floors of toys, the warehouse manager is shaking with rage. "Look, waterboy," he says, "we sent you for beer, not the bloody elixir of life. You certainly took your time, you really did!"

And the goods handler adds his two cents worth: "Hey, Kafka! When's your Uncle Adolf going to die again? Seems he's been passing away in installments."

"Any day now," I say, and I take the invoices and spend the rest of the day double checking and ticking off two consignments of children's toys: one foot soldier with rifle; one soldier in rowboat; one soldier with helmet; one officer, marching; one general in overcoat; one drummer; one trumpeter; one French horn; one large drum; one soldier, prone, with rifle; one artillery gunner with ramrod; one officer, erect, with map ...

I check off the figurines and think about how they're always mistaking me for someone else. I've been living on my own for years now, but the moment there's a pool of vomit anywhere, or someone makes a racket at night, the neighbors come rushing over and give mother an earful. That young upstart of yours was raising a ruckus last night. Does he really get such a kick out of it?

Gunner with rangefinder; one man with telephone, taking notes; one motorcyclist; one wounded soldier, supine; two medics; one doctor in white lab coat; one ambulance dog; one prone soldier with cigarette; one dragoon on horseback ...

My aunt died at the Maryseks, and the next morning Mrs. Marysková hurried over to mother's and complained that I had pounded on the window that night and my aunt was so startled she probably had a fit before she died. It was definitely my fault, because Mrs. Marysková ran out and heard my awful cackling laughter, even though it's been years since I've lived at home.

One cow, grazing; one cow, mooing; one calf, standing; one colt, grazing; various piglets; one cat with ribbon, standing; one chicken pecking; one tiger cub; one spotted hyena, one bear on hind legs; one American buffalo; one polar bear cub; one monkey, scratching ...

Once, I watched a vet bending over a sick calf and telling the owner he'd prescribe an infusion, but then the vet yelled at me to come over at once and take this brush and scrub between the cloves of the animal's hoof, like that, then he insisted I take the brush handle and swab out the creature's mouth, like that. I could only stare at him, unable to bring myself to say I was a bystander, not a stable hand.

One mountain goat; one wild boar; one shepherd boy; one farmer; one chimney sweep; one cowboy standing; one Indian throwing a lasso; one large rabbit sitting; one boy scout in a hat; one sheepdog ...

I entered the synagogue, and a mud-spattered Jew leaned over to me and whispered: "Might you also be from the East?" I nodded. Later, when I stopped off for a beer, two fellows were sitting there and one of them said to me, "You're a baker!" and I nodded, and the fellow rubbed his hands together and said, "See? I could tell right off!" He called for a deck of cards and said, "We need a third for a game of *mariáš. Betl* for a crown, *Durch* for two.... Low card deals."

One Mary; one baby Jesus; one Joseph; one wise man standing; one black wise man; one shepherd with lamb; one angel; one Bedouin; grazing sheep; one sheep dog ...

I check off two consignments of toys at the Zinner Brothers on Maislová Street, wholesalers in toys and fine leather goods, which is why I love to go walking after work, though I'm always tripping over the toys that have passed through my hands that day. I like walking through Kampa Park where children on all fours scrawl chalk drawings on the asphalt pavement, and they continue their drawings up the walls of buildings, as high as they can reach. I'm struck by a picture of a man whose hat has been drawn simultaneously front and back. His hidden ear is sketched above his head like a question mark, like a coat of arms.

"Did you draw that?" I ask the little girl who has just finished drawing it. Her elbows are blue, the color of shotgunshell casings.

"Yes, but it's nothing," she says. She uses her foot to erase a portrait that wouldn't be out of place in an art gallery. "Would you comb my hair for me?"

"If you'd like," I say.

The girl straddles the bench, then tucks one leg under herself, while I sit behind her. She hands me a comb over her shoulder and I comb her hair, and she half closes her eyes. Then she looks at a falling leaf and says, "That leaf's hands are sore, so it had to let go."

Darkness descends rapidly and cyclists wind their way down the serpentine pathways of Petřín Hill with miners' lamps on their heads. Small boats ply the jade water, with every stroke they lift a dozen aluminum teaspoons from the water. A blind man walks past the row of benches, following the radar sweep of his white cane.

"What do you think about when you draw on the pavement?" I ask.

"The way that bird over there sings," she says, pointing into the branches. She lowers her chin to her chest. She's still a child, but in five years, a beautiful parasite will awaken inside her, full of pungent matter with a hint of borax, and gradually flood her life with happiness. I comb her hair, weighing the thick, soft tresses in my hand, then I tie it up with a ribbon. The little girl puts her hand out and very precisely places her finger on the first knot so I can make the second and finish it off with a magnificent bow. Then she turns around, undoes the cord tied around her waist, tightens the two ends of the rope around herself, sticks out her little tummy, and I put my finger on the spot where each end of the cord crosses so she can make a knot and then a bow. And then, in a flash, she kisses the back of my hand and is gone.

From Kampa Park, Charles Bridge looks like a long trough

in which pedestrians appear to be gliding along on roller skates. Prague, its broken ribs in the river, moans in pain. The arches of the bridge vault across the water like hounds on the hunt, leaping from one bank to the other. I could visit my cousin in the brewery, or go back to my landlady, who's invited me to join her for a bottle of blueberry wine, but I'd rather just walk as the spirit moves me.

On Malá Karlová Street a shopkeeper stands in front of his well-lit shop, under a sign with his firm's name on it: Alfred Wieghold.

"A good evening to you, Mr. Wieghold," I say, and in my mind, I ask his forgiveness for staring at his prosthetic hands, as chipped as the hands of the Black Madonna of Częstochowa.

"Looks like rain," I say, and I can't take my eyes off his artificial arms.

"Young man," Mr. Wieghold says, "why do you go walking past my shop on your hands? Put them in your pockets. Experience those pockets to the full."

And he bursts out laughing, this king of marionettes, drumming on his shop window with his artificial limbs, both arms creaking like a weathercock in an autumn wind. Then I walk down Michalská Street, and see a sign that says: "The Iron Door: Strengthens one like fortified wine."

In the passageway I look into a watchmaker's shop and see an apprentice sweeping the floor. He keeps blinking, and his eyes are crusted; he must have conjunctivitis, and I'll bet he has to pry his eyes open every morning to find his way to the washbasin.

Today, I'm encountering walkers in series, as if they were connected by an invisible line: ten people with bandaged heads, a dozen pedestrians with eyebrows meaningfully arched, apparently trying to tell me something, seven people with eye patches ...

But it's the women I notice most. The current fashion is enough to drive you mad. Each one looks as though she's just arisen from a bed of love. What do they have under those blouses? Some sort of scaffolding, or a structure of whalebone that makes their breasts poke one in the eye? And the way they walk! A man in a big city needs a wardrobe of fantasies not to want to commit a homicidal crime of passion provoked by all that trumped-up beauty. At this point a man falls in beside me and starts telling me about the many strange jobs he's had: how he worked in Prague's first automated cafeteria, the Koruna, and how he had to sit concealed inside the contraption and check the one-crown coin people put in the slot, and if it was genuine, he'd put a sandwich on a plate and rotate the mechanism, and he could hear the oohs and ahhs of astonishment at this wonderful invention; or how he had sat inside the huge clock at the exhibition grounds and, with a pocket watch in one hand, he'd push the big hand forward once every minute. As he told me this, he stood there, still transfixed at the wonder of his life.

"Who are you?" I ask.

"A practical philosopher," he replies.

"Then would you kindly explain Kant's *Critique of Practical Reason* to me," I say.

We walk up Štěpánská Street. Prague, as if on a hydraulic lift, sinks lower, and the practical philosopher's hair touches the place where stars are born. Then he invites me for a grilled sausage, and on the way, on Rybničká Street, he gives me an explanation. Then he makes the sign of the cross over his fly and slaps himself so hard on the forehead that he sets the streetlamps trembling.

"The old lady over there usually has decent sausages," I say.

The acetylene lamp casts its light on the old woman, and Rembrandt comes back from the dead. She rests her hands on her stomach as though she were laying them on the Prodigal Son's back. A single tooth shines in her mouth.

"Gentlemen," she asks, "is it midnight yet?"

The practical philosopher lifts a finger to the sky, and in that instant he is as beautiful as Rabbi Loew, or as Vincent's severed ear. The night is full of black slag, silver pinwheels, nuts and bolts. It is redolent of ammonia, sour milk, the intimate toiletry of women, essential oils, lipstick. The clock on Štěpánská Street begins to sound the stroke of midnight; other Prague clocks chime in, then those that are running behind. The practical philosopher eats his grilled sausage with gusto, then walks away without a word of farewell.

A prostitute ambles by, resplendent in a white dress, like an angel; she turns, the pod of her mouth splits open, and two rows of white peas come tumbling out. I long to etch colorful words into her smile, hoping that next morning she'll read them as she stands before the mirror, her toothbrush in hand.

"Ma'am," I say to the old sausage seller, "did you ever know a Franz Kafka?"

"Oh my Lord!" she says. "My name is Františka Kafková, and my father, a horsemeat butcher, was František Kafka. Then I knew a headwaiter at the station restaurant in Bydžov who was also called Kafka," she goes on, leaning closer, her single tooth gleaming in her mouth like a soothsayer's. "But sir, if you'd like something extra, I can tell you, you're not going to die a natural death. Have yourself cremated, deed me your ashes and I'll use you to polish my forks and knives so that something splendid will come of you, like a gift, like misery, like love, hee hee hee ..." and she turns her sizzling sausages with a fork.

"I also read cards," she goes on, "and sir, if you weren't surrounded by a little cloud, you'd make beautiful things.... But go on! Get out of here! ... Here it is again!" she cries, sweeping something off her skirt and kicking it away with her foot.

"What was that?" I ask.

"Nothing. It's just Hedvička, the countess's daughter who drowned. It's her spirit ... d'you see? She's always with me, and now she's tugging at my apron. D'you understand?"

"I understand," I say, backing away from the circle of light cast by the acetylene lamp.

Then I headed home. At the entrance to the Turandot someone is trying to persuade the doorman that he's got money. At the Šmelhaus, music is coming out of the cellar, along with two old men, laughing. Kožná Street is full of obscene signs and movements. A red rose is lying in the gutter, as though fallen from a bouquet. I sit down beside the fountain in the Old Town Square and my shadow is green and outlined in purple. Someone is carrying a large cactus, each nodule tied with a red ribbon. A lady who looks as if she has stepped out of an Ibsen play is walking along Paris Street, wearing an overcoat over her pyjamas. She clearly can't sleep and is on her way down to the river to lean on the balustrade and gaze at the water. A man has just propped himself up against a streetlamp, as if listening to serious music; then he vomits and the liquid runs out of his mouth as though he'd dropped a pocket watch on a chain. I see light in my windows, the curtains billowing, my landlady pacing back and forth, crossing herself. No doubt she has her Bible open on the table propped up against a cooking pot. A traffic cop has emerged from Dlouhá Street, looking as though he'd plunged both of his forearms in plaster of Paris.

I'm thinking of you, my Poldinka, remembering how you told me: "You I hate least of all. In your saliva, I taste a bottomless pit excavated by love. In your teeth, I touch a wall dripping with sadness. Darling, you had salami for supper, because I have a piece of meat on my lips, but it doesn't matter; kiss me and kiss me again, and again chew the flesh around the hollows of my eyes, around the chasm of my mouth. And say it again, that even Solomon in all his glory was not arrayed like this, nor are the birds of the air, nor the lilies of the field as comely as I. Say it again and again. Ignite fiery sacrifices between my legs, set my loins aflame. And when you go home in the morning and see a dress hanging in the window, think nothing of it. It's just me embracing a building charged with sweet memory. They say you can still feel the lost needles of sunlight in the railings."

That was what Poldinka told me back then. We were strolling down to the river where the city walks on its hands. I wondered then why the cars were driving along the river upside down, their wheels in the air, as though sledding along on their roofs, and why passersby greeted each other as though they were scooping water into their hats.

Poldinka said, "Where do you find the strength to deal in those idiotic toys, toothbrushes, and combs, and still have such wild dreams?"

I said: "Poldinka, you alone have understood the words

with which I have inundated your mouth, your hair, the air in your lungs: tiny words plucked from the evening papers. Poldinka, you alone have always known when the wick in my eyes has been trimmed, you alone understand what will remain when I depart, my face leaden and unhearing, because like you, I have never wanted to take my pleasure by the book; like you, I have never wanted to forfeit my right to pain and grief.... But why Poldinka, you perverse, deviant, degenerate woman, why do you bring panic into my life, like a stalactite, like a vampire bat?"

I jump up from the bench in the Old Town Square. A policeman is standing in front of me, his legs apart, his sleeves dipped in quicklime. There's no one around, so I confide in him.

"From this day on, I will never again be free of the desire to walk with the Aramaic professor of laughter, you know? From now on, I will never be rid of the cracks in my brain, because to be free is a joy. And so I'm drowning in happiness itself – in weddings, in pleasure – as I work at the Zinner Brothers, checking off turtle doves, Easter eggs, souvenir chapels, angel hair, Christmas decorations, toys. Do you understand? We are all brothers, brothers in *l'art pour l'art*, as beautiful as *entartete kunst*, as truthful as a nightingale, as perverse as a rose. Do you really see what I'm saying? You can't live without cracks in the brain. You can't rid yourself of freedom the way you'd rid yourself of lice, brother. Do you understand?"

The policeman's reply was harsh: "Don't carry on like that, Mr. Kafka. Why are you shouting? You'll end up with a fine for disturbing the peace."

Strange People

A steel chain, each link polished by proletarian hands, sparkled in ribbons of sunlight that poured through the louvers of the ventilation tower running the length of the factory hall. The chain was hanging from a motionless overhead crane, and the crane operator was dozing in the gondola, her white forearm stretched along the ledge of the cab, her bleached blonde head resting on her elbow. A shaft of sunlight bisected her head and arm.

The shift foreman, Podracký, walked down the hall through band after band of light, as the sun cast stripes on his coveralls. He walked through section three, then section four, moving through blue twilit tunnels, then emerging again into clear, diagonal swathes of light pouring through the half-open louvers.

Now he walked past silent grinding machines and their carborundrum discs, dangling idly from dusty chains. The grinders were sitting on benches by the sorting table; some were reclining on slanting planks, knees up, their arms folded behind their heads, like extras waiting in the wings for their cues.

"If I understand your message correctly," said the shift foreman, "you don't intend to continue working. What exactly do you think you're up to?"

"What you did to us flies in the face of the principles of comradely conduct," said one of the grinders, nicknamed The Dairyman. He stepped forward. "You're just like the kids who write 'Kilroy was here' on the wall and then run away."

"In other words, you're on strike," said the foreman, raising his eyebrows.

"No, we're just not going back to work until we can talk to the person who's meant to negotiate these new quotas with us, according to regulations."

"Right, then. I'll send round the shop steward," said Podracký, and he pulled out a yellow folding ruler, measured the sorting table, refolded the ruler and walked away, slapping it against his thighs to the rhythm of his step. The overhead crane began to move toward him, drawing closer as the blonde operator propelled the vehicle through the shafts of light. She pushed a lever, and, as the crane advanced down the hall, its trolley simultaneously moved across the gantry, the hoist descending on its glistening steel chain. The operator's ample bosom rippled as she passed in and out of the bands of sunlight. The crane passed over the grinders' heads.

The Judge brought a helping of blood pudding from the canteen for the senior worker. Then he went back to the pickling vats, where slabs of steel were soaking in hydrochloric acid. He accidentally stepped into a puddle of spilled acid and began to feel the liquid silently working away. He heard his shoe laces snap, so he rested his foot on the rim of the trough and watched as the fabric of his twill trousers began pulling apart. He looked up at the pile of scrap. A welder was patiently cutting his way into the innards of an old Wertheim safe with a blue oxyacetylene flame. Past him, on the scrap heap, some female convicts were unloading freight cars filled with rusty crucifixes taken from village churchyards. Working in pairs, they grasped an iron crucifix at each end, then swung the corroded symbol of Christianity straight into a waiting hopper. Then they loaded the hoppers up with the charred remnants of tanks, iron railings, ornamental grave markers, swan-like enamel bathtubs, sewing machines, congealed wrench sets, all of it scorched by incendiary bombs, because such raids in World War II set the earth itself on fire.

The Judge reached up and grabbed the control pendant hanging from the trolley and pressed a button, but the hoist moved off in the opposite direction.

"Stop it, doctor, stop it, or we'll crash it into the gondola!" shouted Vindy, the assistant.

The Judge pressed the button, and the hoist came to a halt. Now all he had to do was press the other button. The hoist inched forward, and the Judge followed it along the wobbling boards. Gripping the pendant like a coachman holding the reins of a four-in-hand, he vanished into a greenish cloud of acidic vapor and reemerged on the other side.

"That's it," said Vindy. "That's far enough." The Judge pressed the button. This time, it was the right one.

On the scrap heap, the female convicts slid open the door of a freight wagon, and fire-damaged gramophones tumbled out, sparkling with teardrops of blue glass, remnants of window panes that had melted when the factory was hit with phosphorus bombs.

"Very well," said the Frenchman, "but what if we get crappy material, and the entire ingot has to be ground down?"

"It's all been speed-smelted," said the grinder with a cruciform scar under one eye. "Last time they fired up 'Daniel,' they played music at the furnaces to celebrate the fourteen charges they pushed through in twenty-four hours. That broke the record for a Siemens-Martin, but one of the rollers says to me he'd have all those fuckers and their bright ideas up before a judge, because the billets they rolled from those famous fourteen charges? Half of them had to be scrapped and sent back for resmelting."

"This place is no very nice at all," said Ampolino. "At night, the girls here all go to sleep. Me, when I finish this work, I go home. At home, the girls don't do nothing, and in the evening they all sing and make love. Hey, Frenchman, you agree wit' me?"

"Go home," said the Frenchman, "and don't pay attention to what nobody says. Me, I figured this place was my new country, but I was wrong. I had to leave home because I got mixed up in antigovernment politics, but where I am gonna go now? We can make a living here, boys, but we can't make a life. Out in the world people still know how to have a good time. In Singapore, in this little theatre, I see them let a pony have a go at a black girl. Or Shanghai? I see them boil a monkey alive and he goes crazy from the pain and it scrambles his brains, makes a tasty appetizer. Or Cuba? They let kids fool around with turtles before they kill them, and the kids poke their eyes out and the soup is ooh la la. And back home in France? At La Canebière, in Marseille, you sit around at tables and they have these crazy nonstop shows on a rickety stage, and you can get naked and so can your girl, then you put on these masks and get up on the stage and do it in any position you think of and the audience sitting there at the tables cheers you on ... but look who's coming!"

Vindy leaned over the vat and vanished into a cloud of turquoise vapor. He could be heard scraping away at the slabs of steel with a wire brush, and his voice was audible: "Okay now, your honor, just lower that hoist down and we'll hook it up to the sling. The slag's already been eaten away."

The Judge, trusting to beginner's luck, pressed a button, luckily the right one. The tackle descended into the sickly green vapor, and he heard the hook clank against the sling and the metal basket containing the slabs of steel. Vindy leaned over the vat, and only his trousers were visible.

"Far enough!" he commanded.

The Judge, like the king in a puppet show, released the controls, leaned into the acrid vapor, and fed the hook into the sling from the other side. But he couldn't keep his head over the vat and straightened up abruptly. He emerged from the vapor holding his arms in front of him. All his mucous membranes were seared and burning; he was blinded by tears and he felt the acid making his nose run.

But Vindy, the assistant, whose membranes and sense of smell had long since been destroyed over the pickling bath, pressed the button, and the hoist raised the basket out of the vat. Hydrochloric acid ran off the slabs of steel, releasing more of its acrid fumes.

"They're clean!" he shouted.

They turned and watched a tiny figure slowly approaching down the length of the long factory hall, lashed as he went by golden swatches of sunlight, as though he were walking beside a picket fence floodlit from the other side.

The man stopped and planted his hands on his hips. "Look here, comrades," the shop steward said, "the imperialists are closing in and there's no time to waste. We have to pour the molten steel of peace down their bellicose throats ..."

"Hey, Václav," said the Dairyman, "we've all read today's editorial in *Rudé Právo*, too. There's a different issue here. Why don't you consult us before you raise the production quotas? Whatever happened to proper procedure?"

"All very well," said the steward, squaring his shoulders, "but what you're doing is called a strike."

"What if it is? The constitution allows us to strike. So yeah, constitutionally, we're on strike. We're not working until the one who's supposed to negotiate higher quotas shows up."

"But there's a war on in Korea right now," said the steward, raising his voice. "Pusan is about to fall. For the last time, are you going to get this shuttle moving?"

"No, we're not!"

"All right,' said the steward, "I'll have to report this to the manager," and he walked away, while the louvered ventilation tower cast stripes of light, like a prison uniform, across his back.

A breeze carried away the veil of greenish vapor, and Vindy leaned over the stack of metal slabs, while the Judge removed one of his gloves and placed his hand on the wet steel.

"Your honor," said Vindy, "wipe that stuff off right away! Give it a rinse, quick!"

The Judge hurried along a tottering plank, turned on the tap, but then he slipped and fell up to his crotch in a space between the board and one of the hoppers. He quickly freed himself, though he could tell he'd injured his knee, but he rinsed his hands and looked over at the scrap pile just as a young woman wearing a prison uniform appeared. Her left arm was in a fresh cast, and with her right hand she grabbed an ox bridle, carried it to the hopper, and tossed it in, just as the other convicts were about to add the last of the crucifixes.

"And a-one, and a-two and a-three," cried a female voice.

The crucifix arced through the air, and one of the convicts jammed the figure of Christ hanging from it into the pile of scrap with both hands.

"She's doing time for going over the hill, trying to escape the country," Vindy explained. "Yesterday she got her arm caught in something. But listen here, do you know that when Nezval was just a kid he dragged angels into his poems?"

"Say again?" asked the Judge.

"Maybe he's a Jew," the assistant went on. "Seems to me these days his poetry exudes the spirit of the synagogue, of the Antichrist. They say that when he was born the Archangel Gabriel stood over his crib. So if he doesn't believe in Gabriel, why did he drag that angel into it?"

"No idea," said the Judge, "but it seems to me that the acid has all drained off."

"Right, so I'll just shift the load a little. But I'm going to have to dispel the shadow of Freemasonry myself," Vindy said, spitting out a long string of saliva. "I'll write a poem and call it 'How Brother Victor Ahrenstein Carved a Block of Stone by Proxy.'"

"Boys, he's going to throw the book at us," said the Restaurateur.

"No, he won't," said the Dairyman. "If we don't get any satisfaction, I'll go see Poncar. And if he won't help, I'll go straight to the top, to Tonda. Wasn't it Tonda who taught us to stand up for our rights as workers?"

"If someone wants you to walk a mile with them, walk two," said the Priest, "and if he asks for your shirt, give him your coat as well...."

"Yeah, and if someone strikes you on one cheek, turn the other," the Dairyman interrupted him. "Good advice for a saint, but a worker? If he doesn't go straight for the solar plexus, he's doomed."

"We've already turned the Church upside down, and there's more to come," said the curly-haired Cop.

"Maybe that's just what will get the Church back on its feet," the Priest said.

"Maybe, but I'm telling you, in fifty years, there'll be nothing left of the Church but the churches."

The Sergeant Major got to his feet, opened a notebook to the sunlight, and said, "Lay off, the holy father here is the only one who's got his head screwed on, but today, I'm going to have to put a big fat zero in my notebook, because that's exactly what they'll pay us for just standing around. So, Mr. Prosecutor, how much time could we be looking at for this?"

"I'm working on it," said the State Prosecutor, pacing up and down. "They could hit us with the Defence of Public Order law. That one has bigger maximums."

"But the law's on our side," said the Dairyman.

"It might be on your side," said the State Prosecutor, "but it's not on mine, because I was tossed out of my job. Of course, if I were still a prosecutor, I could turn all this into a nice little antigovernment conspiracy. I'd accuse myself of being the intellectual mastermind behind this strike, and, as an additional incriminating factor, I'd add that as a former state prosecutor, I knew it was a crime and should have reported it. . . ."

"But this is Kladno!" the Dairyman thundered. "We're totally within our rights! We all work here – defeated classes, communists – we're doing all this so we'll all be better off!"

"I wouldn't be so sure about that," said the Cop. "Before they tossed me off the force, we operated on the Dual Punch Theory. That is, it always depends on who hits who. If a worker slugs a prosecutor, they can lock the prosecutor up because the presumption is he provoked the worker into doing it. But if a prosecutor slugs a worker, even if the worker was asking for it, they'll throw the book at the prosecutor because . . ."

"All well and good," shouted the Dairyman, "but you can't get away with that in Kladno! You just can't!" The overhead crane was approaching, its chains clanking.

"Yes," said the Judge. His trouser leg had now split open to the knee. He took off his shoe and shook the rest of the cloth loose, as if he were removing his underwear. He looked at the scrap pile where the female convicts were loading another hopper with iron coffin lids. They brought over cast-iron angels with corroded wings and faces – angels splattered with blobs of scorched clay – and tossed them all into the hoppers.

Vindy held the control pendant hanging from the traveling

hoist in his hands. He walked along the planks behind the moving basket filled with the slabs of steel and held forth: "The thoughts of Itzak Mauthner, sitting at the *comptoir* in his central office in Náchod: In the spring of 1830, an Ashkenazi Jew from Halič named Mauthner came to Náchod and declared, That house over there will be mine. In 1832, Mauthner the homeowner declared, That factory over there will be mine. In 1839, Mauthner the manufacturer said, I have five knitting mills and I wish to own nine. And thus the firm of Mauthner's Knitting Mills came into being, a concern belonging to an industrial overlord with no family escutcheon and no traditions, a magnate who, when he bequeathed his industrial kingdom to his sons, had no idea his sons would shroud themselves in the anonymity of a publicly traded company and that the sons of those sons would become press barons."

Vindy pressed a button, and the crane came to a halt above a freight car on the tracks. A string of silver saliva emerged from his mouth, which he wiped on his spittle-soaked sleeve.

"It's as easy as pie," said the Judge.

His shoe began to open up like a water lily.

The crane operator moved through the flickering bars of golden sunlight and into the tunnel of shadows. At the far end of the long factory hall, the crane had seemed tiny but it drew nearer like an aircraft with broad wings and came to rest above the yard engine and the group of grinders. In the gondola, a man in a black-cotton smock – the manager – stood up, planted his white hands on the gondola railing, leaned over, and with a golden sash of sunlight across his chest, spoke as if from a cathedral pulpit.

"Honor to work!" he said, using the official party greeting.

"I'll honor work if the pay's decent," retorted the Dairyman.

"So, comrades, we have a plan, and we have to get on with it," the manager said, stabbing downward with his finger. "Otherwise I'll have no recourse but to report you to the union council."

"Who ordered the higher quotas? Who consulted with whom?" asked the Dairyman.

"The Ministry of Heavy Industry."

"At whose suggestion?"

"At ... at our suggestion."

"There, you see, the fox is in the henhouse! And the ones you should have consulted first you never consulted at all. What are we, just a bunch of statistics?"

"No, I was merely executing a trade-union decision. Now, are you going to get back to work?"

"No, we're not. Only if you personally put it up on the board that we're operating under the old quotas until we get a firm agreement, negotiated as per regulations."

"Right, then," said the manager, raising his black sleeve till it was immersed to the elbow in a shaft of golden sunlight. "But I'm reporting this to the director's office and to the trade union."

"Why are you treating us like this?" shouted the grinder with the cruciform scar under his eye. "Why are you taking a day's wages out of my pocket?"

"Václav!" said the manager. "I hardly know you any more. You're an old comrade and you're coming after me like that?"

"You're making my life miserable!" the grinder shouted, and he picked up a crowbar, tossed it from hand to hand, scattering little reflections of sunlight around the shop, then hurled it at a stack of cast-iron slabs. The crowbar clanged and clattered to the ground, the echo of its voice dying away among the blue shadows. The grinder ran on to the stack, climbed over the slabs, quivering with rage, and stood there, sliced in two by a band of sunlight.

"But Václav, I'm one of you, I'm a worker too, you know that," the manager said, placing his hand over his heart.

"Then you should understand what this is about," said Václav, and he walked to the opposite side of the shop; the gate groaned open, then slammed shut.

The manager threw up his arms and nodded at the operator, who pushed a button, and the crane moved back through the factory hall carrying the manager away in the gondola, his back to the men, while the sun pouring through the ventilation louvers whipped his black cotton smock with golden scourges.

The vapors rising from the pickling vat were unbelievably beautiful and dense. The Judge couldn't resist. He walked quickly across the plank and thrust his arm into the cloud up to his elbow.

The female prisoner squatted down on the scrap pile, cradling her wounded arm in her lap like a plaster doll and, with her good arm, she picked up an angel – the kind that used to decorate horse-drawn hearses or aristocratic gravesites – and she carried it to the hoppers.

Vindy handed the control pendant to the Judge and indicated its proper use. "Your honor," he said, "we use this button to raise the load, and this one to lower it. This button is for moving the load forward, and this one is for moving it back. We can't afford to get them mixed up, so let's try again. Yesterday, I wrote a poem called 'Ministerial Night: In Which the Departmental Head Has a Vision of Tantalus at Five Minutes to Midnight.'"

"Thank you," said the Judge, and took over the controls.

"Or," Vindy asked, "would you rather hear my poem called 'How the Miner's Daughter Forgot Her Proletarian Origins and Succumbed to the Temptations of Eros?" But then he caught himself. "Oh God, I'm always going on about myself. How are you doing, your honor?"

The Judge pushed a button, but it was the wrong one. "Stop! Stop!" Vindy shouted.

The Sergeant Major took a piece of chalk and wrote the number twenty-two on the gate, followed by twenty-eight, drew a line under them, wrote down the difference, and underlined it twice. Then, tapping the chalk on the result – six – he turned to his listeners and said, "They want us to crank through an extra six hundredweight a day! But what if each ingot needs a complete grinding!"

At that moment the gate slid open, and the Sergeant Major, still facing his listeners, tapped his chalk on the forehead of the man who'd just opened it.

"There's a film crew here, boys," said the maintenance man, the chalk still poised on his forehead. "They're looking for workers to have a discussion about current events."

"Well, in that case, let's go," said the Dairyman, and, with the other grinders, he walked out into the sunlight where a van was parked. Some of the film crew were unloading buckets of whitewash. The young director pointed to a wagon loaded with ingots, and the cameraman carried his camera across the rails.

"I hope it's not like the last time they tried to make a movie in the steelworks," said the Frenchman. "Everyone was gone home for the day, so the film guys had to bang on buckets and drop tin cans from way up to make factory noises. They talked all enthusiastic about completing their plan."

"Here's a good spot," said the director. "Just slap some whitewash on that wall, and then we'll set up the aquariums with some fish in them ... a spot of greenery over here; make it look like a birch grove ... and you," he pointed at the grinders, "you guys want to be in this, right?"

"Thanks for asking," said the Judge, stopping the hoist. "Ever since they evicted me – and it's a wonder they didn't lock me up – I've been doing wonderfully. Do you know, my rheumatism has completely vanished?" He pushed the right button this time, since there was no other choice.

"I don't suppose you'll be sending the authorities a thank-you telegram," said Vindy, and he raised his glove and gave a signal.

"I won't," said the Judge, "but somehow, I've become a simpler person psychologically." The chain with its shiny tackle descended into the cloud of greenish vapor rising from the hydrochloric acid. "Before, I used to drive everywhere. Now I take the streetcar. I used to drink imported beer – Bernkasteler or Badestube. Now I drink Kozel from Velké Popovice. Instead of going to the club, I go to the warming hut, and so on.... In tens of thousands of years, mankind hasn't essentially changed. The thing is, my friend, I was neither prosecutor nor defence attorney. I merely listened and drew my conclusions from the two sides arguing their case before me. You know, I'm still as keen on Dreiser and Picasso and Chaplin as I ever was, but today I'd put my landlady up against any of them. Every morning, she dresses three children who are still half-asleep and drags them off to the nursery and toward evening she picks them up and brings them home again. To me, that woman is a greater piece of work than the Dove of Peace, or *Monsieur Verdoux*, or *An American Tragedy* . . .

"What if your landlady were a communist," said Vindy, ejecting a thread of silver spittle from his mouth. "What would you say then?"

"But that's precisely what she is, and how!" said the Judge, bending over and brushing the remaining bits of slag off the slabs of iron. "I know what I'm talking about, my friend. My parents ran a boarding house and had seven children."

"Well," said the Dairyman, "we won't tell our mothers anything, and then we'll take them to the movies and surprise them."

"Right, then," said the director. "Sit around on these ingots, some of you lean against the wagon, one of you hold this map and pretend to be pointing something out, and the rest of you read the newspaper. When I give the signal, you'll all start pretending to have a lively discussion about what you've just been reading."

One of the film crew pulled some freshly cut birch saplings out of the van and began arranging them, while the director motioned him to shift the branches to the right, and then a bit more to the left, and then forward a bit, perfect!

"It'll be just like the Feast of Corpus Christi," said the Restaurateur.

"In other words, you've been saved," said Vindy and he leaned over, whisking off the steel slabs.

"You could say so," said the Judge, while the acid gnawed away at what remained of his shoe. "Now I live alone in a tiny room. I call it my submarine room. Every day I bring bits of wood home from the factory – leftovers from broken crates, small pieces of Russian birch they packed the Russian chrome in, Norwegian oak veneer from the ferrosilicon crates, sometimes pieces of German fir from the nickel crates – and then I sit at home in my submarine and the walls are sweating from the humidity, and I sit there as if I'm in a sauna and stoke the fire with Norwegian and Spanish oak and German fir and watch until the flames have consumed everything ... then I gaze into the dying embers until the warmth is gone and all that remains is an amorphous-looking structure. Sometimes I bring back pieces of wood with company names branded into them, stoke the fire, and the letters no longer make sense. . . . I gaze into the open stove and watch the flames licking away at Fiskaa Norway ... Metalwerke Saxonia ... Made in Yugoslavia ... Meeraker Sverige ... the fire dissolves and scrambles the words and their meaning and in the end, everything just burns up and is gone. . . . And I think how wonderful it is to have been forced into this situation. . . . I'd never have had the courage to do it myself," said the Judge. He lifted his head from the cloud of greenish vapor.

"What do you do on Sundays?" asked Vindy, as he maneuvered the hook into the sling and then pushed the button.

"On Sunday my landlady dresses up her three children,

and I take them for a walk through Julius Fučik Park. They let me keep one good suit, so when I go out walking, I'm still Judge Hasterer out to take the air. But most of all, I enjoyed living with my daughter. When they moved us out, we got a room that was one sofa length each way. We called it The Chapel. Every morning, we'd comb the plaster out of each other's hair, and the soles of our feet were covered with plaster too. The main waste pipe for the entire building ran right through the middle of our tiny room, so every time someone flushed a toilet or let water out of the sink, we'd hear it cascading down past us. There was a bathroom next to where we slept, and the taps were right where our heads rested against the wall. If our neighbors got up before we did and turned on the taps, we'd both have the same dream – that water was pouring out of our heads. And there were other nice things about our little chapel. There was some kind of research institute next door where we could hear gigantic machines drilling or cutting up enormous pieces of steel all day long, and I'd imagine that our little chapel was a giant tooth being endlessly drilled by a huge dental drill, and, do you know, it made my molars ache."

As he was talking, the Judge walked along the boards behind Vindy, who was pushing the steel along in an iron barrow.

"The acid's fagged out," said Vindy. "Time for a new demijohn."

"Let's do a brief rehearsal," said the director, looking at his watch. "We still have a shoot in Chomutov. You take the map, that's it, open it up, and you, open the newspaper ... and when I signal the rest of you to shout, 'Americans, go jump in the ocean!' I want you," he said, pointing to the Prosecutor, "to say 'That'll be the day!' in a skeptical tone of voice."

"Not doing it," said the Prosecutor, raising his hand. "I'm in enough trouble as it is. If anything's going to help me out here, I'd rather say, 'Yankee go home!' "

"All right, that's perfect. 'Yankee go home' it is," nodded the director. "Now we'll do a couple of framing shots, and then we'll go straight to film. It's going to be called *Lunch Break in Our Factories*."

"But we're not eating anything," the Priest objected.

"Then get something," said the director.

"We've already had our lunches. We can pretend to drink from empty cups, like the chorus of musketeers in *Dalibor*, but a salami sandwich would ... "

"Absolutely," said the director, rolling up his sleeves. "But time's flying. Move the aquariums up against the wall, and meanwhile, go buy yourselves some salami and rolls."

"You buy it, and expense it," said the Cop. "Aren't we worth it?"

"Jesus!" sighed the director, rolling his eyes.

Vindy pointed the way, then jumped up on the edge of the vat and down the other side. The Judge, holding the control pendant, followed after him with the hoist.

"Stop! Stop!" cried Vindy.

The Judge pressed the button, but it was the wrong one. There was nothing he could do but press the right one.

"You'll get the hang of it," Vindy said. "But tell me about some of the other times when you were happy."

"When I'd go to the small paint factory next door for firewood. They let me have old aniline-dye barrels – purple, red, green, blue, yellow – and I'd bring them back to our court-yard and chop them up. My hands got stained with whatever color had been in the barrel, and I'd touch my face and the back of my neck, and my daughter would laugh at me and say I looked like a parrot. Then we'd have a fire in the stove, and each time the flames were a different color."

"Does the little yard engine that makes all that beautiful smoke go by here?" asked the film director,
"Every hour."
"Damn! That would have made a great backdrop! But go and fetch some plates, and I'll send for salami and rolls."
The assistant director brought in some apprentice steel-workers and coached them for supporting roles in *Lunch Break in our Factories*. One group was supposed to look at the aquariums with interest and talk to each other about the fish, while the second group would emerge from the birch grove, run up to the workers in the middle of their discussion, and sing the popular motivational song, "We'll Command the Wind to Blow and the Rain to Fall."
The director took a piece of chalk and drew a diagram on the gate of the scrap-metal division. He and the assistant director choreographed the shooting plan. The gate slid open, while the apprentices stood around watching, and the director, chalk in hand, tapped the forehead of a man in an English-style suit walking through the gate into the sunlight, along with the factory manager in the black smock, and the shop steward in dirty coveralls.
"Right, we're ready to go live," the director said, and the

grinders emerged from the factory hall with empty mugs and pails and picked up the salami and rolls in their free hands, and some opened their newspapers and sat leaning against the ingots while a group of apprentices bent over the aquariums looking at the fish, and the rest took up positions behind the little birch grove.

Vindy gave a signal and the hooks descended, clinking against the demijohn's green glass.

"And now, a little something from me, Doctor," he said, clearing his throat. "A poem to the great Jaroslav Vrchlický: No region lay beyond the reach of thy poetic soul on thy vasty pilgrimage through life. In verse, you made our history manifest, the obverse and reverse of all our eras, and thus, in winged words, you elevated and elated us, your brethren . . ."

As Vindy recited his piece, the senior worker arose from his plank in the little shack, kicked the door open, then sat down, looking through the window at the pickling vat shrouded in its cloud of greenish vapor. He cut his blood pudding into sections, counted them, carved himself an equal number of bread slices, then skewered a piece of blood pudding and a slice of bread with his knife, thinking how comical the Judge looked standing there, and wondering if he was confused about the buttons on the control pendant only because he, the senior worker, had been mean to him and whether it wouldn't be better to try to get on the Judge's good side because he was, after all, a judge, and the whole damn factory – all of Poldi Kladno – was full of people from professions and jobs and trades of all kinds, and the whole working-class character of the steelworks had gone down the drain, and the conversations you heard in the changing rooms were something else these days, a lot of eggheads had come in, and it was the same in the canteen, the guy in coveralls was really a colonel or maybe even an attorney general, and we had to be nice to them, because was it their fault that they ended up on the losing side?

"Action!" said the director, raising his arm, and the camera whirred; the grinders munched on their sandwiches, shouting at each other with their mouths full: "The fortress at Pusan is about to fall! Jump into the sea, you imperialists! We're going to pour the molten steel of peace down your gullets!" The apprentices pointed at the fish, and the group emerging from the birches danced along the tracks, singing: "We'll command the wind to blow and the rain ..."

"Cut!" said the director. "And now we'll do a medium shot from above."

He helped the cameraman climb up on a wagon loaded with ingots, and the assistant carefully handed the camera up to him.

Again, the camera whirred, and the grinders rattled their empty dishes and shouted slogans, and the apprentices ran out of the birch grove and leaned over the aquarium again, until the director waved his arms and said, "Cut! That's it – we're done! Thank you!"

Vindy's voice carried high over the acid vapors: "Greatest among poets, you sang the praises of our meadows and entered the pantheon of the Muses, Jaroslav, to join the company of giants. Today, your footsteps lead to glory everlasting ... though not for everyone ... for in these times, caught in the onrush of daily cares, we've spurned your legacy, oh master, or yet because the fleeting glory of this gilded age has blinded us. . . . E'en so, with each new spring the orchards garb themselves in blossoms new, and our spirits do ascend once more from chaos unto order . . ."

Vindy removed his cap, revealing hair as thick as a lambskin hat and a head so large that the cap had to be slit at the back and refastened with a large safety pin. The senior worker emerged from the wooden shack, spat out a piece of blood pudding that had lodged between his rotting teeth, then stepped across the boards and walked past the hoppers and through the cloud of greenish vapor. When he emerged from the room where the demijohns of acid were stored, tongues of green vapor were licking at his coat and trousers like tiny flames.

Across the tracks came the manager, the shop steward, and the man in the English-style suit, who in the meantime had put on a worker's cap.

"This is the Trade Union rep, in person," said the manager.

"He made the time – tore up his busy schedule, in fact – to come to see you personally," said the shop steward.

"Look here," the union man said, "I've learned with great regret that you're not on board with the notion that we must all work to bring socialism closer to fruition." And because he saw in himself a reflection of the president and First Citizen, he tugged his cap further down over his forehead. 'What would the author of *Red Glow over Kladno* say if he heard about this?"

"Good question," said the Dairyman, raising his empty tankard. "What would Tonda Zapotocký say if he knew you're having us meet quotas you haven't negotiated with us according to regulations? Tonda was never against us! I was just a boy when he played the accordion with my dad, and in the evenings he taught the workers never to give in."

The union rep turned around, took two steps, reached into to the aquarium, scooped up some water, and dabbled it on his forehead as though anointing himself with holy water. Then, in a fascinated tone, he said, "What kind of accordion was it?"

"A Helikon," said the Dairyman, "and he'd go for a drink with my dad to Secka's. Tonda was a mensch."

The union rep took the map from the Priest's fingers and studied it. "You can't talk that way," he said. "You're playing into the hands of the aggressors. If I'm not mistaken, I heard you say during the shoot that you all understood quite correctly that Korea is bleeding and needs our weapons. But what am I hearing now?"

"Exactly the same thing as the shop steward here and the manager heard," thundered the Dairyman, "You're treating us like little boys, and that's a dereliction of party morality! What the hell's going on here?" the Dairyman shouted, pounding his tankard on an ingot.

The union rep glanced at the shop steward and the manager, leaned delicately against the aquarium, studied the little red and golden fish, then turned around. "But you can't behave this way," he said wearily. "We can't be talking back, we can't be disobeying government directives."

"Then, comrade, you should take it up with comrades Krosnář and Zápotocký, because they taught us that the ones upstairs are there to listen to us down here. 'Face to face with the masses,' wasn't that the slogan?" The Dairyman waggled his hand, then turned to the grinders, as if expecting each of them to agree.

The Judge jumped up on the edge of the vat, holding the lines of the control pendant like the reins of a four-in-hand, his white legs protruding from his disintegrating overalls. He walked behind the hoist from which the green demijohn full of hydrochloric acid was suspended. Encased in wicker, the demijohn hung in the air like a green moon. When he saw the senior worker, he teetered for a moment on the rim of the vat like a tightrope walker, but then walked on, pressed the button on the pendant, and brought the hoist to a halt.

The senior worker nodded. "I see you're getting the hang of it," he said.

"Indeed," said the Judge.

Vindy placed a steel bar across the mouth of the vat, raised his hand, and the Judge pressed the button, the right one, lowering the demijohn. Vindy kept his hand in the air until the demijohn settled on the bar and began to tip. He uncorked the neck and the greenish, acrid liquid bubbled into the vat, while the demijohn kept tipping until it was upside down.

"But this plays straight into the hands of the reactionaries," said the union rep. "By the way, we've heard that the former owner of an industrial bakery in Kladno gave his daughter a million crowns for a wedding present. How can that be, I ask, when we all started out with five hundred a month?"

"You're missing the point, comrade. History will swallow this baker up. Maybe he sold his house and his fields. Maybe he had diamonds and gold coins stashed away. But enough of this, boys," said the Dairyman, raising his tankard. "Enough! Comrade, you've got our shop steward here, and our manager. Just work it out with them the way it's meant to be done. Send the production manager down here to negotiate the higher quotas directly with us. Even if you don't know the proper party guidelines, I do. We know very well what the government needs. Come on, boys, let's go for a beer. There's no talking to this secretary here, not yet anyway."

He lifted his tankard and walked off, followed by the grinders. When they reached the tracks, they looked around, and the Dairyman turned to the film director and his men, who were just climbing into the van, and said, "What you just heard? That's what you should have made your movie about, you peckerheads. The aquarium and birch trees would have been perfect."

The union rep watched the gang of grinders leave and gave a weak little smile.

"I'm telling you," whispered the shop steward. "The comrades here in Kladno are sharp as razors."

"Who the hell was that?" asked the union rep, as the manager slid open the factory hall's gate.

The female convicts were taking a break on the pile of rusty crucifixes and angels and some other pieces of scrap. The yard engine pulled the loaded hoppers off to the smelting ovens and returned with empty ones. One prisoner with a stoop found some loose metal pickets, handed one to another prisoner, and assumed a fencing stance; the other prisoner faced her and they began making ridiculous lunges at each other. The prisoner with the stoop was driven back up the pile scrap by her opponent, who forced her over the top of the pile and back down the other side, while the other women hooted, clutching their sides, hugging each other, hanging on each other's shoulders like dray horses resting against each other on lunch break, roaring and howling with laughter.

"I'm going to die," shrieked Lenka.

"Here's what I know," said the shop steward. "The Dairyman – we call him that because he owned a milk bar, but he voluntarily shut it down and went to work in the mines, then came here as a grinder – he's our best worker and a dedicated communist but what can I say? He's a Kladno boy. When a mother's in the pink, none of her children want to fetch her wood and water, but when she's sick, the children fight over who gets to help out first, if you catch my drift."

"When she's sick, when she's sick ..." said the union rep thoughtfully. "But when she does get sick, that might also be too late, don't you think?"

"Girls! Girls!" the young guard said quietly, standing there, pale and ashen-faced, his fingers hooked into his Sam Browne belt.

At a signal from Vindy, the Judge pressed the right button, and the demijohn turned upright again. The Judge then continued along the edge of the vat, pressed the proper button and the demijohn moved on through the acrid vapor.

"Very good," said the senior worker, and he smiled.

Vindy walked over the wobbling planks to the demijohn

and into the cloud of vapor now enveloping Judge Hasterer. "Things are improving in the realm of the spirit!" he shouted.

The crane clanked along the length of the hall, and the sun was already so low in the sky that the ribbons and bands of light from the ventilation tower had shifted from the walls to the ceiling, where they glowed like golden sword blades. The crane pushed its way through blue shadows and semi-darkness, and the load binder raised his arm, his blue coveralls blending in with the blue shadows in the hall. He stopped the union rep, who put his finger to his lips and watched as an old worker lifted up a crowbar, lay it against his cheek as if aiming a rifle, and when the crane operator drew closer, he shouted: "Bang!"

The union rep watched the blonde operator fling her arms in the air as though she'd been winged, then lay her bleached head on the edge of the gondola, sagging for a moment, and then gently rising to her feet, rattling the chain. She laughed at the worker as her crane rumbled over his head.

"There are some strange people here," the union rep said, as he turned to watch the crane recede down the factory hall. "So, just to be perfectly clear," he said, and he looked a moment longer at the receding gondola, then put his arms around the shoulders of the steward and the manager and stuck his head between them. "First, send the production manager down here right away to negotiate the higher quotas. Next, put a message up on the board that the old quotas apply, for now. And third, how old did you say this Dairyman was?"

At that moment, the public address system started broadcasting a waltz, and the female convicts tossed aside their pickets. They converged on the wagons and began dancing with each other on a patch of hard clay. The girl with her arm in a cast ran down as well and, lifting her cast in the air, embraced it with her healthy arm and waltzed with herself.

"She's one of them defectors," said the senior worker.

"That, sir, is my daughter," said the Judge, bowing slightly.

"Now girls!" said the pale, somewhat alarmed guard. "Girls!"

The Angel

The young guard stood outside the room where they stored fire-clay piping. His thumbs hooked into the Sam Browne belt supporting a holstered revolver, while he watched the female prisoners unload the large fire-clay conduits. Beside him a willow tree – its pussy willows stripped by human hands each spring – was struggling to recover. The guard gazed at the mountain of wartime scrap; at the piles of fire-blackened metal hospital beds, gutted x-ray machines, cardiographs, and other medical devices; at a stack of disabled typewriters, the consequence, he assumed, of a direct hit on a typewriter factory, their keys grinning in the sunlight like teeth in a dead man's skull. Scattered among the mangled letters were tiny beads of greenish glass, the remnants of windows melted in a fire-bombing that had consumed everything, even the cobblestones and the very air itself. A child's crib sat on top of the pile of typewriters, and fixed to the metal headboard was a colored tinplate print depicting a little girl in a white dress walking across a chasm on a narrow footbridge. Hovering above the girl, almost touching her back with its hands, was a guardian angel, also in white, with two large wings, like twin brides. The young man's complexion was pale, and he had deep creases, like knife scars, on each side of his mouth. He stared at the picture, took out a pocket watch, paused a moment, guessed it was one o'clock, then looked at the dial, but as usual he was half-an-hour off. Two workers in aprons pushed a dolly into the storeroom and began to stack it with the fire-clay conduits the female prisoners had unloaded.

"Sir," said one of the prisoners, whose name was Lenka, "these guys have got to lug that stuff a long way. Couldn't I give them a hand? We're done here."

"Nice little angel," said the guard, pocketing his watch and pointing at the cot.

"My nice little guard," Lenka said, pointing at the guard. "Have we ever tattled on you?" she whispered, touching the sleeve of his uniform.

"Go ahead then," he shouted. "And the rest of you! Sweep out those empty wagons!" He was yelling at them, but the women knew he felt badly about it.

"Thank you," said Lenka, and she walked into the shade of the storeroom, her raw linen trousers and white blouse moving through the shadows. Four alluring convicts hopped into the wagon and began singing quietly: "A single day without you in my sight, is like a year of everlasting night...."

The guard turned back to immerse himself in the colored tinplate on the cot sitting atop the pile of leering typewriters, and when he tugged at his Sam Browne belt, it was as if he could feel the strap tightening over a pair of wings and crushing the feathers, and he realized that his comrades in the unit had nicknamed him "the guardian angel" for a reason.

"Need a hand?" asked Lenka.

"If the Angel okayed it," said the Atom Prince.

"Let's set up a human chain," said Mr. Hulikán.

"A good-luck chain. But please, take off your gloves," said Lenka under her breath.

"Flesh to flesh," laughed the Prince.

He took the conduits from the pile and handed them to the girl. As she took the sharp-edged objects from him, she lightly brushed her finger against his palm, and when she passed them on to Mr. Hulikán, she caressed the back of his hand as she let go.

"It's awful!" said Mr. Hulikán. "These days, when I get paid, I don't know if I should just chuck the money straight into the stove or blow it all on booze."

"Save it up," said Lenka, "and when I've done my time, you and I will go on a little spree."

"By the time you're out of here," said Mr. Hulikán, "who knows where the hell I'll be? But explain this to me. For fifteen years I delivered ice around the pubs, and in every pub they gave me all I could eat and drink. Not only that, on a good summer I managed to stash away enough cash to buy six pairs of shoes and six cartons of cigarettes." Mr. Hulikán said this angrily, and as he bent over the dolly, Lenka kissed the top of his head, right where the part ran through his thick hair.

"At least you're getting paid," she said.

"You're still just a filly," said Mr. Hulikán, his voice rising. "But I'm the wrong side of fifty." He hitched his trousers with his elbow, although they weren't slipping down. "When I worked at the Orion candy factory, for lunch I'd put almond chocolate and cream into my lunch bucket, then I'd blow some steam into it and whip it into a froth. Add in a cookie and voila! And the parties we had! We had a skeleton key to the storeroom where they kept the liqueurs. When they changed the locks, we'd take an empty liqueur barrel, pour hot water into it, swish it around, and the hot toddies had us crawling on our hands and knees. Today? Look where I've ended up! I only make enough for food and booze. Where's the room for my family in all this?"

Mr. Hulikán quickly took two fire-clay conduits from Lenka and set them down on the dolly.

The guard leaned against the broken willow, staring at the cot on the pile of typewriters. The angel drew him into the picture, pinned wings on him as big as twin brides, and gave him the satisfaction of knowing that he too had taken someone under his wing, a female prisoner who had gotten pregnant on the night shift through the barbed wire during last year's cold snap – not by him, but by a certain man on the other side of the fence. The barbed wire had damaged the tendons in her knee and cut her buttocks, but through her tears her eyes were glowing. Then last fall, a gypsy girl had scraped a hollow in the earth on her side of the fence, and a man who may have been a gypsy as well, but in any case was very determined, hollowed out the earth on his side, and got her pregnant. It had been raining hard, and the only remaining evidence was a cavity under the fence and finger marks scratched into the wet clay. He had seen the gypsy girl afterward, still covered in mud, but with radiant eyes.

"Prince," Lenka said under her breath, "pretend you've got

something in your eye." She raised a bleeding ring finger and daubed the young man's index finger with blood.

"I've got nothing in my eye," said the bewildered Prince.

"Don't be stupid," said Lenka, stomping her foot. She was trembling. "So tell me," she asked, "what's new in the world?"

The Prince continued taking conduits from the pile and passing them on, and each time, the prisoner caressed both pairs of the men's hands, while three pairs of work gloves lay discarded on a nearby plank. A copy of the *Daily Worker* was sticking out of the Atom Prince's coveralls, and he patted the pocket, saying, "Nothing special, except a little girl named Bessie Smith went to show her doll to the black welterweight world champ, Sugar, who lived in the Central Hotel, and the little girl never made it home."

"Did anything happen to her?" asked Lenka.

"Matter of fact it did. Her guardian angel walked out on her," the Prince continued. "It says here they found little Bessie in the bushes not far from the Central Hotel, strangled with a silk scarf, but the welterweight world champ couldn't remember a little girl by that name among his admirers. Scotland Yard launched an investigation, but – oh, I've got something in my eye!" the Prince yelled. He dropped the fire-clay cylinder and began rubbing his eye.

"He's got a sliver of metal in his eye," Lenka said, coming out of the storeroom. "May I help him get it out? May I?"

"Do it!" yelled the guard. He watched her walk away and saw himself following her, holding his hands close to her back, and he felt a surge of angelic energy flowing between his protecting hands and her protected back, like the picture on the cot, and he saw himself, when the shift was over, shepherding the female prisoners across the wooden footbridge over the classification yard, and he could already hear the feathers dropping from his wings, as large as twin brides but tightly bound by the Sam Browne belt that held his revolver.

Mr. Hulikán, smoking a cigarette and looking sour, sat on the dolly that was neatly stacked with fire-clay conduits. Lenka cradled the Prince's curly head in her arms, lifted his eyelid with her thumb, and held him close.

"You have beautiful eyes," she murmured.

"Yeah, sure," he said.

"Be nice to me, just a little. Jesus Christ, I need a man, merciful God, I need a man," she whispered, her breath hot.... "Tell me what else is new in the world," she said out loud.... "Now look up – that's it."

"The Americans have landed in Korea," he said, "but they fired MacArthur, which is too bad, because he wanted to drop the atom bomb."

"Now look down," she said, pushing her knee between the Atom Prince's thighs. "Dropping the bomb would make you feel good?"

"You're not kidding," said the Atom Prince.

"What about the people down below?" she asked, pushing her knee higher.

"The more the merrier."

"But people are people, aren't they?" she murmured, and a tiny bead of sweat broke free, rolling down her forehead. "Now look to the right – that's it. The girls wanted to know how Zátopek did in the race yesterday."

"A national disaster," said the Atom Prince. "It was a

crowded race, I'll say that. At first Schade, Pirie, and Chataway led the pack, while the ace runner, Gaston Rieff, kept moving up. But after the eighth lap, nerves began to fray. Zátopek sprinted for the lead, the way he always does, but then Mimoun pulled ahead, worse luck!"

"Did Zátopek lose? We were all rooting for him!" Lenka said. She pulled out her hankie and ran the corner of it around the inside of his lid.

"Zátopek's a cunning devil," the Prince said wearily. "He shot ahead at the last minute and set an Olympic record."

"Oh, that's beautiful," Lenka whispered, her body shaking as though she were working the treadle of a sewing machine. "That's so good."

"You know, the Americans tested a hydrogen bomb in the Pacific that's a thousand times stronger than the one they dropped on Hiroshima," the Prince said.

"Enough about the Americans," she said. "I've had it with them. All their talk about how we had to stand up to the communists got me into prison, and last week they brought in a trainload of Swedish ore that we had to shovel out of wagons marked 'American Zone of Occupation' ..." She sighed and shuddered. She didn't even notice that Mr. Hulikán had flicked his fourth spent matchstick past her head. He'd lit another cigarette and was still sitting on the edge of the dolly looking at the ground, as though he were butting heads with destiny. Then he tossed away his cigarette and jumped down.

"My guardian angel's abandoned me," Mr. Hulikán said. He walked out of the storeroom, repeating to the guard: "My guardian angel's abandoned me! Used to be I either got paid in kind, or I stole what I needed. But here? I was better off doing piece work in the Šumava forests. At least we had enough to drink. The Rusíns taught me how to pour a few gallons of denatured alcohol into a shallow well and light it on fire, and then, at just the right moment, smother the flames with blankets.... It turned the well into a source of drinkable hooch. But the final straw that got me into all this shemozzle was when I killed the dray horse that I used to deliver the ice with my fist. They fired me. And that's when my guardian angel left me high and dry," Mr. Hulikán said, speaking directly to the guard.

"It's out," cried Lenka, and she exited the storeroom bearing the nonexistent mote from the Prince's eye in the corner of her hankie; she gave a deep sigh that rose from her very toenails, while the other female prisoners went on sweeping out the wagons. But the guard heard nothing; he was leaning against the warm boards that covered the outside of the storeroom, pondering his sins of omission. As he stared at the colored illustration on the child's bed, he imagined himself on bitterly cold days, a white angel, leading the female prisoners at the end of their shift downstairs to the men's shower room; there he would let them warm themselves by the radiators while they stared at the walls, casting sidelong glances into the corridor as the naked steel workers emerged from the changing room carrying soap and towels, and the women stared at the naked male bodies, following them round the corner with their eyes, and those eyes became showerheads showering the bodies perfumed by dust with their desires. As the guard wrote his daily report he felt the prisoners' blushes become his own and he knew that what he allowed to happen was against regulations, but he felt it was more important to show the people in his care, at least once a day, something like a Christmas tree ...

"Keep moving!" shouted the guard. "Rinse out those soup buckets, and then wait for me!" But the prisoners knew from his tone of voice that he regretted having to say it.

When the prisoners were leaving and the workers began pushing the dolly loaded with fire-clay conduits out of the storeroom, the guard climbed up the pile of typewriters, pulled down the cot, and with a pair of metal snippers he'd borrowed from the welder, he cut the colored illustration from the headboard. He took the picture with him into the storage room, looked around, and behind a pile of fire-clay piping, he unbuckled his Sam Browne belt, took off his tunic, and slipped the guardian angel under the back of his shirt, its wings against his shoulder blades. Then he put his tunic back on and pulled the belt tightly over it so he could smuggle the picture out through the factory gate. When he emerged into the sun and ran to catch up to the women, walking behind them as their guardian, he felt the wings in the tinplate picture merging with his body, and he knew that neither his Sam Browne belt nor anything else in the world could prevent him from having wings of his own as big as twin brides, that nothing could prevent him from continuing – inadequately and against regulations – to protect the women in his care. And that, in his own mind, was his salvation.

Ingots

At the very edge of town the door of the public house flew open and the publican dragged out a girl with long fair hair and tried to shove her down the steps, but she grabbed the banister with both hands and yelled into the night: "Let me live! Let me live!"

The publican wrapped an arm around the girl's waist and, with his free hand, took out a bunch of keys and struck her over the knuckles, and when she released her grip he kneed her in the back and she stumbled down the steps, her arms flailing. She collapsed in a heap on the empty roadway, her hair splayed like a peacock's tail or an ostrich-feather fan.

"Hey, there," shouted the Prince, "how do you know that's not my girlfriend?"

"Some girlfriend, you piece of shit!" said the pub keeper, turning in the doorway to face him. "She put away nine rums and five beers, and she can't pay the tab." And he slammed the door behind him, locking it angrily.

"Let me live!" cried the girl.

A fire truck in full cry roared past the railway tracks that ran through the scrap-metal division of the steel works. Some firemen were sitting on jump seats, others stood on the running boards, their helmets glistening in the morning sun. One of them had a gleaming white set of teeth and stood with a boot propped on the front mudguard. He was hanging on with one hand and saluting with the other, gazing around him with a celebratory air, acknowledging the accolades he imagined coming his way and announcing to no one in particular: "The cooling pipes in the blast furnaces are clogged. We've got to douse them with water."

"Things are getting much better, doctor," said Bárta, the loader. "Christian Europe is consolidating."

"Which Europe?" asked the doctor of philosophy derisively. "And what d'you mean 'Christian'? It's more Jewish than ever before."

They were pulling scrap out of the railway wagons and loading it into hoppers: cylinders and pistons, a glass disc, the crushed remains of Leyden jars, twisted compasses, metal hoists with weights and counterweights, a bundle of iron rods and electromagnetic coils, an upright galvanoscope, a spectroscope, and a sextant with mirrors. Bárta, a former merchant, removed brass components from the scrap and put then into a box so when the shift was over, he could take the brass away and sell it for cash.

"It is Christian," the merchant said.

"That's crap," said the doctor of philosophy, raising his hand. "At one end of the spectrum you've got one brilliant Jew, Christ, and at the other end you've got another genius,

Marx. Two specialists in macrocosms, in big pictures. All the rest of it is Mother Goose territory."

He took a jimmy and pried loose the latch on the next wagon; then he and Bárta lifted the door off its hinges and gently let it slide down to the tracks. They climbed inside and started rummaging around. They brought out a sump pump, an old blower, pieces of a threshing machine, a farm gate that had been dismantled with a cutting torch, a paper cutter, a seed drill, a field mower, an old weigh scale, and parts of a plough. They tossed it all into the hopper.

The Prince knelt over that lovely head of hair, but as he bent down, he fell over on his hands. For a moment he remained on all fours, then sank in a heap on the road and rolled onto his back, gazing at the sky, while the stars spun around like a tree in full blossom. He rolled over on his side, righted himself unsteadily, and felt burning alcoholic bile seep from his stomach into his mouth.

"I've got nowhere to sleep," the girl wailed.

"We can put you up," said the Prince. He crawled toward the prone figure, pushed her hair aside, then sat up and fumbled in his pocket for matches. He found them, but each time he struck one it went out. Finally he managed to ignite a sheaf of four together, and he could see her face in the flare. Her eyes were open, and when she turned toward him he could see a long scar running across her forehead, jumping her eyebrow, continuing down her cheek, and ending at her mouth.

"When I was little I had a pony," she said, "but no one believed it was mine."

"I believe you," said the Prince, and he stood up, quickly planting his legs apart to keep from falling over again.

The girl sat up, got to her knees and then to her feet, wavering unsteadily.

"They don't know what to do with me ... my endocrine system ... it's like I've got a chest full of jelly ... they keep giving me injections," she said, struggling out of her coat.

The Prince took a step, lurched forward a few paces, then stopped, his legs apart.

"First we got these b-b-bubbly little sores on our skin," she said and started walking after the Prince, dragging her coat in the dust by one sleeve. "See, I'm working with really toxic stuff now.... I package iodine salts. I'm covered in it." She pushed her hair back with her hand, looking up at the sky and making a circle above her head with her arm. "I'm covered in sores, like the sky."

She set off at a trot, got ahead of the Prince, then stopped and turned to face him.

"Where do they get all this stuff?" complained the merchant. "So long after the war and still so much scrap."

"Just so there's no doubt about it," the doctor continued, "the Jews nailed it down: Freud in quackery and art, Einstein in physics. Two more specialists, but masters of detail this time, microcosms. A foursome of brilliant Jews, and the entire world stands on their shoulders. The rest is all just warming up the soup and watering down the vodka."

He took a pitch fork and began heaving things straight from the wagon into the hoppers next to it: chains, rusty ploughshares, yokes, sugar beet hoes, seed boxes, and tubes from planting machines.

"What about America, eh?" yelled the merchant.

"Oh, right, America," said the doctor. "They're sitting pretty now that Morgenthau and Baruch are on the Atomic Commission, and all they did was dither until the Russians got the bomb too, thank God."

"But the Americans have more bombs," said the merchant.

"That's for sure, they do have more," the doctor nodded, "but that cow, Peroutková, really got up my nose when she said that the Americans bombing Prague at the end of the war was just a teensy little foretaste, and that this time around it would be a different kettle of fish. Listen here, Peroutková, you silly cow, fuck your Radio Free Europe, because what kind of a life will I have if you blow it to smithereens?"

He raised a finger and just where he was pointing – beyond the piles of old war material, where the domes of the blast furnaces towered over the landscape – he could see four silver streams of water shooting into the air, showering the furnaces as if they were taking part in a fire drill or a training exercise at the firefighting academy. A cloud of blue and pink steam poured off the furnace walls, then quickly dissipated and was lost against the blue summer sky.

"Any chance of a smoke?" she asked.

The Prince staggered to his feet and steadied himself while he patted and poked about in his pockets; then he sullenly handed her a pack of cigarettes. When he struck a match, the girl leaned over the flame and her hair fell around it as though she were inhaling it. She smoked hungrily and the ember glowed in the dark, illuminating her face through her hair. She broke into a stumbling run, as if driven forward by the alcohol, then she had to slow down while the

Prince trudged after her, fighting an urge to run backwards, as though someone were dragging him to a place he didn't want to go. They climbed a narrow pathway beside a ditch carrying wastewater from the mine. On the hilltop, they were dumping slag that cast a red glow and blue shadows over the landscape. The girl's hair shone like pink cotton candy. The Prince lit her another cigarette.

"That's quite a scar you've got on your kisser," he said, walking along the edge of the ditch.

"There was this craaaazy family back home," she said, and ran several yards ahead of him, then she turned and went on. "They called themselves the Colorados and claimed they were nobility, but all they had was this little shop.... When they'd go to the district fair they'd ask the railway to add on a saloon car, just for them.... One of them was truly in-in-insane and when I was a little girl I'd ride my pony and tease him by calling him Count Colorado!"

The girl was shouting, but the landscape was silent now. A baby carriage was approaching down the path with a small, bright blanket inside it. As it passed them, the Prince saw that the woman pushing it was in tears. Wrapped inside the blanket was a whimpering little dog.

"What's up, Mum ... what ... what happened?" he asked, steadying himself again.

"My little Haryk got hit by a car, poor dear," the woman said as she passed by. "I'm taking him to the doctor's."

"Count Colorado!" the girl shouted, waving her crumpled overcoat. "He was a madman. Once he came after me with a scythe and whacked the p-pony's hind legs with it, and I fell off into a patch of nettles, and as he was backing away, he

didn't see me and ran the tip of his scythe across my face."
The girl yawned and started running again, stumbling over
her coat.

The professor of philosophy climbed into the wagon, hand-
ing the merchant the scorched components of a grain hopper, a drum separator, sifting machines, a grain sorter, and a
device for whipping cream.

"Looks like a mill must have burned down somewhere,
eh?" Bárta said, tossing the items into the hopper.

"All our good old golden days are being smelted down, and
you don't even know it's happening," said the doctor. "This
age we live in has stunned you like a calf in a slaughter house,
and what are you doing? You're tossing into the furnace the
very things, the very means of production, that created your
class in the first place . . . and you're completely unaware of it."

"But the world won't just leave it at that," laughed the merchant. "Look at Iran – they're fighting back tooth and nail."

"Iran?" asked the doctor.

"Yeah, Iran."

"You're mistaken," said the doctor. "You mean Iraq."

"No, I listen to Radio Free Europe – Iran."

"Look here," said the doctor, "they're all pricks and pis-
sants but there's still a huge goddamn difference between
Iran and Iraq. However, my friend, the Russians are here,
and that's what matters. They've always had good chess masters, bass players, weight lifters, wrestlers, speed skaters and
foreign policy."

And the doctor set an ice-cream maker and a meat grinder
on his apron-covered knee. With gloved hands, he picked up

a meat chopper, some ladles, a cylinder head from a compressor, a slaughter-house stun gun, some bone splitters and turning hooks, and he carried them to the edge of the wagon, where Bárta took them and tossed them into the waiting hoppers.

They were standing by the fence around the barracks. The Prince yanked out two boards and they slipped into the compound, the girl bending forward, her hair over her face, yawning. He held out his arm to indicate she should go ahead, but as he did so he staggered backwards, hit the dormitory wall, and slumped to the ground.

Inside, Karel the fireman was looking into the mirror, baring his gleaming set of teeth and brandishing his axe. He had his helmet on and gazed at himself through half-closed eyes. He wore tight-fitting calf-high boots, and from the moment he'd first pulled them on, he felt utterly sure of himself, decisive, the same way he felt when he wore his big belt.

The door to the room swung open and he spun round, alarmed to see no one there. The volunteer workers were all asleep in their bunks, except for Jarda Jezula, who lay on his back, fiddling with a bunch of artificial roses wired to a slat in the bunk above him.

A drunken worker with deep circles under his eyes sat backward on a chair, toying with a glass of wine and watching its reflection flicker across the table top. "Concentrate," he mumbled. "Think of it, say it at once, and you've got it. What am I afraid of, Marion?"

The fireman braced himself, walked over to the doorway and shouted into the dark corridor, "Don't play games with me! You'd better watch out! My case officer'll tell you what a dog I was in reform school!"

The Prince stepped through the doorway, turned around, and held out his hands to draw the girl in from the dark. She stumbled into the room, bent over at the waist, her hair dishevelled. She tossed her coat aside, and the fireman jumped up on a chair; the reflection from the wine glass on the table top came to rest. Her arms outstretched, the girl collapsed facedown on one of the bunks and her hair spread out like spilt milk.

"But there's humanity here," said the merchant. "There are ideas here."

"Humanity, my friend? We saw that in the slammer; that's where humanity is now. Nothing but rat finks, maniacs, bottom-feeders, and big mouths with raging paranoia! All we ever heard inside was, 'I'll show the fuckers the minute Zenkl shows up from Cheb on a white charger!'" The doctor of philosophy was shouting, his eyelids hooding his eyes. "Humanity will forgive you if you're a horse's ass, but if you speak five languages, they'll never let you live it down, especially not in the slammer. There was one particular swine who was doing time for politics, like me, but he liked to play the coachman, get on his high horse, and he'd grill everyone who came in, even though it was none of his damned business. He pointed his whip at me and asked, 'So what are you in for?' and I said, 'I'm ashamed to tell you,' and he gave me a taste of his whip, so I said, 'I fucked a goat,' and he ate it up. 'Out with the details,' he said, and I said, 'It was a goat, but she was pregnant, and I ripped her open, so they threw the book at me.'

After that the son of a bitch left me alone, but I had to stay sharp, because one day he was about to let a wagon roll over my foot, but luckily it stopped when the tongue got caught in a crack in the stairs. I was ready to punch him in the face, a real whopper, right on the nose, but then common sense got the better of me – you know how it is – all the ones doing real time were absolute masters of mayhem. But some day, I'm going to let someone have it, that's for damned sure, and they won't know what hit them." And he went on, dragging the scrap out of the wagon with a bent pitchfork: rusty saws, bandsaws, chopsaws, crosscuts, Swede saws, rip saws, keyhole saws, cog-wheels, spindles, bobbins, needle holders, a set of rusty drills, some axes, hammers, grinding wheels, compasses, charred carpenters' adzes.

"Boys," said the Prince, struggling to get his boots off, "I brought you a sweet little piece of ass."

"You're the man," said the fireman, climbing off the chair, "I'll go first."

"Jarda, are you having a go too?" asked the Prince.

Jarda merely smiled beatifically.

"Forget about him! Haven't you heard?" asked the fireman, and he knelt beside the sleeping girl and flipped up her skirt. "Jarda's fell hard for an ex-pavement pounder. Today was her name day and he carries a bouquet for her across the whole damn steel works ... and she burst into tears." In a single motion, the fireman ripped off the girl's panties and tossed them at the wall.

The Prince walked unsteadily to the table, opened a drawer, took out a pair of scissors, then went to the bunk.

"Getting their clothes off is always a pain in the ass," he said, then he cut through the hem of her skirt and with a sudden jerk, ripped it in two. "That's hard work," he said, stumbling back to the table. He sat down on a bunk. "Jarda," he said, "you used to be a bit of a hound. Don't you want a little taste?"

He pointed at the helmet, which appeared to be resting on the girl's head, at the fireman's uniform now blanketing her body, at the axe shaking rhythmically on the fireman's back.

"Think your girl is any different?" the Prince asked.

"I'll say she's different," said Jarda, and he went on fiddling with the plastic roses, "but she used to be like that ... and anyway, do we know who that is under Karel? Maybe she's somebody's sister. Somebody's daughter for sure. Maybe she's your future old lady. Your wife, the woman you maybe have kids with."

"You slimy scumbag!" the Prince shouted.

"But the intelligentsia's still around, they'll put an end to all this," said the merchant.

"That'll be the day," said the doctor. "Yesterday, when I was getting a pedicure in Jas, I ran into a sculptor friend of mine, who happens to be an old classmate, and he says to me: 'They just gave us a beautiful exhibition space in the old Riding School up at the Castle!' And I say, 'Well, la-de-fuckin'-da! The aristos used to hump their nags around that place, and now you're going to use it to flaunt your art? Couldn't you have put up something different? I'd leave it as a riding school, and if one of those minotaurs drop in to the Castle for a state visit, let him go riding.... Or how about this? Once a week, put a sign up in the Riding School that says, Free Humping Today!' That's what I told my sculptor friend, and he just walked away. I'm telling you, you can smell the shit in the intelligentsia's trousers from thirty feet away these days."

The doctor stood up in the wagon, then jumped down. The two of them took the other door off its hinges and carried the scrap to the hoppers: a metal worker's anvil, a bundle of wagon axles bound with wire, ball joints and sockets, metal-bending machines, blacksmiths' hammers and tongs, a fireplace screen, lock-makers' drills, portable spinning wheels, a base for portable gas-furnaces, polishing wheels, a set of pipe threaders, gun drills, hole-punching pliers, ratchet wrenches, cutters, belt pulleys, manual air pumps, a jack, and the remains of a gantry crane.

The two laborers woke up. First they stuck their bare feet out from under the covers; then they sat up and looked down at the bunk where the fireman was moving up and down, the girl's bright hair surrounding his helmet like a aureola, while her two white arms and legs stuck out from underneath him like a cross.

"Marion, what is this gentleman making love to?" the old worker said, looking at the reflection from his wine glass as it flitted around the tabletop. He brought the glass down on the table with a bang, stood up, pointed to the girl, and said, "She's contemptible!"

"And what about the armies of whores you had when you were younger, eh?" asked the Prince, still struggling to pull his boot off.

"They were merely pitiable," said the old worker. "They all

had jobs somewhere in Teta or Ara that never paid enough, so they had to earn extra. . . . As long as they had their youth, they got by, more or less." He turned around, sitting on the bunk next to the fireman's helmet and the girl's white arms. "We saw those miserable old hags offering themselves for five-crown notes by the Těsnov station, in the park by the Deniska, or that little park at Invalidova, or outside the hospital Na Františku, or in the street outside Kučera's or at the Old Lady ... and there were columns of desperate, lonely people, dragging themselves back at night to their hostels in Kobylis, or at Krejčar's, or at the Jewish hospice, or to the brickworks in Vysočany, and my sister would yell: 'Something must be done for these people!' But we did nothing. We were rich, and watched those parades from the window. And today? Today, she denies everything to my face."

"Fine," said Bárta, the merchant, "but some ideals are still alive, and the aristocracy still subscribes to them. They still know about getting back to the natural order of things."

"Couldn't agree more," said the doctor of philosophy. "They're the only ones who still know how to get back to the natural order of things. An English lord can get plastered and do swinish things as easily as a farmhand, but he does it among his own people, in the club. That's why there are so many clubs in England, and why on the outside everyone's a gentleman ..."

"I meant the Czech aristocracy," cried the merchant.

"Oh, them? As a young boy I remember Prince Šternberk would hold a hunt, and afterward, there'd be an alfresco orgy of eating and drinking. Oh God, I remember the Contessa

Šternberková – how old could she have been? Twenty-two and gorgeous. But in the middle of the banquet, when the aristos were already plastered, the Contessa plants her riding boot, which she was still wearing, on the tablecloth, points her foot at one of the old degenerates, lifts her leg, and farts like an old mother bear. The barons and princes howled with laughter. Their monocles clinked, they guffawed.... *Oh, sapristi! Comme charmante! Éblouissante!* And why not? The Contessa was among her own kind, and she too reverted to the natural order of things. The next day, when she went to church in her coach, she was the perfect Contessa again, with her little nose in the air, which to this day still gives me a vision of the infinite ... and I knelt by her carriage, and she acknowledged my presence with a slight wave of her handkerchief."

As he was speaking, they went on unloading rusty pipe clamps, glass-cutting shears, boxes of soldering flux, carbon brushes for electric motors, a small metal-shaping anvil, a pewter soldering iron, and then, together, they lifted out heavy iron wheels, lateral-toothed cog wheels, camshafts, roller bearings, connecting rods, clutch plates and drive-shafts.

"All right then, what's left? What?" asked the merchant, shaking both hands over his head.

Karel, the fireman, rolled over on his side, caught his breath, and stood up. He straightened his collar in the mirror and cocked his helmet at a rakish angle. It shone like a monstrance.

"Not that great," he said, nodding toward the bunk. "She's like a dead fish. I should have set fire to her hair. It would have gone up like straw."

"But what about the shop girls these days working in the Pearl or the White Swan and those other places? Don't they have to earn extra? ... Are they making enough?" asked the Prince. His boot finally popped free, and he fell backward like a rocking chair, his boot in his hand. "Go to the Curio Bar, or the Baroque ... office girls go there to earn a little extra, maybe help their friends pay the rent – isn't that so?"

"That's a fact," said the old worker with deep circles under his eyes, "but believe me, those girls are to be pitied. This one here is contemptible. If they find her here tomorrow, Prince, you'll have the cops all over you and they'll pop you back inside, no more suspended sentence ... but Marion, what do the stars say?" The old worker walked back to the table, poured himself another glass of cheap wine, and resumed his observation of the red reflection scampering around the tabletop like a piglet on the run.

"What's left?" asked the doctor, and he paused thoughtfully, looking at the four streams of cold water drenching the blast furnace wall. He looked at the workers high up on the furnace, dismantling the elbow joint of one of the cooling pipes that encircled the furnace walls and conveyed cold water that was gravity-fed from the cement cistern high above the steel works to the pipes around the blast furnaces. As the streams of water from the fire hoses doused the furnace, two workers suspended in slings finished taking apart the joint.

"I'll tell you what. I believe in people who are capable of wrestling with their fate," the doctor of philosophy said bitterly. "For me, there's nothing greater than that because ignorance – not knowing – reigns in my field too. The moment a philosopher comes up with a rational explanation of the universe, or of himself, he turns his back on it ... Lao Tzu: the art of not knowing; Socrates: I know that I know nothing; Erasmus of Rotterdam: In praise of folly. Nicolas of Cusa: *Docta ignorantia*, learned ignorance. And what has our precious twentieth century given us? The revolt of the masses! And in art? We're happily regressing to the time of the Flood."

So said the doctor and, with disgust, he flung the objects he'd removed from the wagon into the hopper: farmers' shears, a small hammer, sewing clamps, leather-working tools, a baking oven, a hot water tank from a woodstove, stove plates, a hemp comb ...

"I don't want nothing to do with it," said the fireman, "and if something comes of it, I'm certifiably crazy and I've got the papers to prove it."

The Prince held his head and rubbed his temples. "Well, let's toss her out," he said, and he stood up and shook the sleeping figure, rolling her over on her back.

"Let's hope she don't croak on us," the fireman added, but then he caught sight of himself in the mirror and was thrilled to see how marvelously his uniform suited him.

"Young lady, the fun's over," said the Prince, and he shook the sleeping girl again.

She slumped headfirst off the bunk: first her torso, her beautiful hair sweeping the floor, followed by her two naked legs, like two white fish.

"Then can we at least discuss prostitutes?" the merchant asked desperately.

"Now you're talking!" the doctor of philosophy said, holding up his gloves. "If only there were any left. Go into any nightclub these days, my friend, and you'll feel like weeping. You have to drink some watered-down concoction with a feeble-minded bimbo who doesn't know her assets from her deficits. She can't play the piano, doesn't know what conversation or good fun is. Ah, but when we were part of Austria? The whores at Goldschmidt's, now they were real ladies! I had an assignation with one of them in Stromovka Park, at the Rosebush, and she showed up in a carriage like a countess. Or take the whores at the Napoleon, or, Christ Jesus! at Šuhů's, where three florins would get you a decent look at those buxom pieces of ass – but just a look, no alcohol – three florins, and then the *Schwantzmutter* would say: 'Goodbye, young man, we'd love to have you back again, anytime.' But that we were part of Austria then. After the war, of course, prostitution was beneath a woman's dignity. It was all because of that suffragette bitch Plamínková and Masaryk's sainted daughter, Alice; her most of all. Some army major gave her a bad fuck, or maybe he spurned her, so now the whole world can go without. And from then on, it's been the twilight of humanity.... Jesus!" The doctor of philosophy stood up. He watched as the yard engine approached to take away the loaded hoppers, and he saw the jets of water that had been dousing the blast furnace subside. "One of the whores at Šuhů's," he went on. "Sweet Jesus! When she'd go for a stroll along the Ferdinand Allee, she was something to see, a regular freak of nature, statuesque, relaxed, a kind of Ur-woman she was, and no one could help turning and looking. What was manly in the men would stick out like a bicycle pump ... a woman like that was the absolute spirit of the earth, to put it in Hegelian terms."

"I used to study medicine," she babbled.

"A douchebag is what you are," said the Prince, opening the window. Stars were twinkling overhead. The sky had reached the point where the night was beginning to wane but the morning hadn't yet come.

"Now be a good girl and get lost," said the Prince, pointing to the window.

"I used to work for an information service," said the girl. Her hair was wrapped around her head.

The Prince lifted her up, and then fell down. When he found his matchbox, he took a bunch at once and held them against the striking surface.

"If you don't get out, I'll light your hair on fire," he said.

She sat down, then struggled to her feet, supporting herself on the bunk with her hands, then she tottered to the window and said, pointing innocently, "Through here?"

"Through there," said the Prince. He remained on all fours a moment longer, then slowly rose to his feet.

"Fourteen months in Pankrac prison," the girl said, lifting one leg over the sill and into the cool air. She leaned back into the room and added, "I was supposed to start my sentence yesterday."

The Prince stumbled to the window and pushed her through it with his elbow. Her fall was odd, as though she had been skewered by the windowsill. Her hair flew loose and, as if turning on a spit, she rolled on her own axis: first her head, then her torso, then her legs flew up in the air like a pair of white weasels ... and when her hair and torso had disappeared, her legs followed them into the darkness the way a high diver is swallowed up by water, and the window frame was left empty except for the tense and tingling stars.

"It's all going to work out," said Bárta, the merchant, hopefully. "Just as soon as we get our property back."

"You'll get shit back," said the doctor of philosophy. "Don't you get it yet?" He pointed at the yard engine pulling the hoppers heaped with scrap metal off to the blast furnaces. "Don't you understand that you've been loading all that stuff, the very tools of your trade, into those furnaces, and the ingots that pour out of those furnaces are meant for a different era? A year from now, where will all those small businesses, those crappy little companies, and their machinery be? Gone! And what'll become of you? The same as all this scrap, the tools of your trade ... you'll be ingots too. This new age is melting you all down, because it's not the measles you've come down with, it's the epoch. And what about me? I hope I live to see the rentiers in Paris sweeping the streets, and the communists booting them in the ass. I hope I live to see the blacks in America fucking millionaires' daughters! My only regret is I won't be able to take part in that fuckfest myself, because I'm already advertising a house I no longer want to live in. Farewell, old world!"

The Prince picked up the girl's panties and tossed them out the window, and for an instant the undergarment spread its wings like a purple bat. Then he threw her coat and her torn skirt out as well.

"When I was a little girl, I had a pony ..." she wailed.

Karel, the fireman, adjusted his helmet at a jaunty angle, shut the medicine cabinet with the mirror inside, locked it with a padlock, tested it several times to see if it held, and then, still holding the key, he turned around.

"I was quite a dog in my day, and my case officer can tell you a thing or two, but Prince, you are a dog among dogs."

The Prince took a shiny, handworn whip from the corner and cracked it in the air. Then he picked up a small purse that had fallen out of the girl's coat pocket. He opened it and removed a piece of paper, unfolded it, and suddenly he became sober.

"Well, I guess it's true," said the Prince. "Karel, stop by the police station and tell them you and me and Jarda want to report a girl who was supposed to sign in at Pankrac yesterday to start doing her time. Tell them we're turning her in, because we're all on probation. Everyone'll see we're just covering our butts."

The fireman set off to work, full of the vanity that radiated from his narrow boots, his tightly cinched belt, and the helmet tilted rakishly over his eyes.

The doctor nodded toward the departing yard engine and saw the other workers leaving the scrap metal yard, heading toward the little shack they had erected with advertising panels taken from closed businesses. "Fafejta's Condoms, Guaranteed To Save You From A Life of Need." "Give Your Tastebuds A Boost With An Ego Chocolate Bar." "We'll Buy Your Gold. Best Prices!" "Famira Bras Give Shape To Your Secret Charms." "Suzi The Seer Sees It All In Her Magic Crystal

Ball!" "A Housecoat From Eusner's Will Win Her Heart. Silk, Padded, Double-Stitched. Jindřišská 20." "Kosetek's Permanent Wave: You Look Good, You Also Save!" "Massages, 8 Nekázanka Street: Expertise, Elegance, Discretion." "Please Don't Pick Or Step On The Flowers. They Have Feelings Too." "Get Potential! Sensational Relief For Men Who Need A Pick-Me-Up To Do The Deed!" "Romany Rose Will Read Your Future. Palms, Tea-Leaves, Tarots."

The fire truck roared past the scrap metal division. Firemen in drenched uniforms were sitting on jump seats; some stood on the running boards, their black helmets glistening with water. The fireman with the gleaming white teeth, his boot propped on the mudguard, hung on with one hand and saluted with the other, acknowledging accolades that no one was sending his way and shouting out to the workers: "Know what was blocking the cooling tubes? A little boy, cooked to death! A bunch of brats went swimming in the cistern up there, and the kid got sucked into the intake! They promised us bonuses, and now they're dragging their feet! Can you believe it? An extra crown per hour they promised us and they reneged!"

The doctor of philosophy ducked his head and entered the low structure cobbled together from old billboards and plate-metal signs, with the slogans and ads from nationalized and closed businesses. He sat down among the workers, all of them former businessmen, craftsmen, and professionals. "Greetings, Ingots!" he said.

A former miller, a former owner of a carpentry shop, a former butcher and a former locksmith nudged and winked at each other, and the miller said: "Sit down, old man, and tell us some of your dirty stories."

At that moment, a load of molten slag was dumped onto the slag heap and the sky glowed pink. In the distance, the sleeping town lay steeped in its pre-dawn atmosphere, with its green roofs and bare slate spires. The blast-furnace chimneys loomed in the background, and atop the middle chimney, a gentle blue flame flickered with an amber glow around the edges. The slopes of the slag heap darkened, leaving only a meandering scar of red-hot slag, the landscape's gaping sex.

The stars faded, the tiny ones already gone out, leaving only a few large dying stars shimmering in the firmament.

A voice below the window whispered, "Let me live, let me live!"

A Betrayal of Mirrors

The summer this year was a hot one. Young boys bounced soccer balls off the walls and the screen-covered basement windows, practicing the Czech Wall Pass. The super's wife told Mr. Mit'ánek in strictest confidence that she thought Mr. Valerián had either taken up acting or dancing, or he'd taken leave of his senses. He'd been down there in the basement since early morning with another man, and they were cavorting about, crashing into each other, drinking cheap red wine straight from the bottle, and yelling: "Can't stop now! Must keep at it!" A month ago, she added, Mr. Valerián had brought in vats of ceramic clay, and then the day before yesterday, it was a mortar trough. She had seen him wandering about the basement half naked with nothing more to cover his torso than a piece of dog pelt that he used as a floor mat by his bed, and that other fellow was there with him, with the very same floor mat covering his naked torso. And every day, two women came to visit, both wearing cloche hats decorated with artificial cherries. And these two reprobates in dog skins were threatening each other with axes – old stone axes like the kind Robinson Crusoe made.

Mr. Mit'ánek slipped off his Auxiliary Police armband. In his free time he liked to catch citizens in the act of alighting illegally from streetcars and slap them with fines. "Let me look into it," he said.

He knocked on the basement door.

By the wall of the Church of the Most Holy Trinity, a stonemason stood on a scaffold, repairing the statue of St. Jude Thaddeus, who had lost a knee and an eye to the ravages of the weather. Further down, the wall of the church was covered with plaques, and a sexton was attempting to pry loose the rusty screws holding them in place.

"Dear Lord Jesus in heaven," said the sexton. "I'm sick and tired of these cults."

"It's paganism," nodded the stonemason, removing a sandstone knee and eye from his satchel.

"I almost ripped out a fingernail," the sexton said, shaking his hand.

"Do titles still count for anything in your heaven?" asked the stonemason. He pointed to the plaque the sexton was holding. The inscription read: To Saint Jude Thaddeus, in gratitude for your timely intercession during the storm. Engineer K. H. and Dr. J. "Enamel thank-you notes, and metal missives," he laughed. "Who actually delivers those things up there?"

"Lord Jesus in heaven," complained the sexton, "two hundred and ten of these tablets, each with four screws, that makes a total of eight hundred and forty screws, and I'm expected to winkle every one of them out of the wall with my bare hands. I'm sick and tired of these cults!"

"All it needs is a little common sense," said the stonemason, and he positioned the eye in the graceful sandstone statue.

"But that's not the end of it," sighed the sexton. "Once I unscrew all these enamel love letters, I'm going to have to remount them all on the other side of this wall, inside the church – with these freaking flippers," he said, holding up his delicate little hands. "Another eight hundred and forty screws. Before that, I've got to pound eight hundred and forty holes into the wall with a star drill, and then hammer in eight hundred and forty wooden plugs. These walls are like concrete, for heaven's sake, because didn't the Church have to build everything to last to the end of bloody time?"

"Come in! I'm the artist's aunt."

A bony hand beckoned Mr. Mit'ánek inside.

"I'm an auxiliary policeman," Mr. Mit'ánek said, bowing his head slightly.

He entered the basement studio. A fire was flickering in the stove. The artist, Mr. Valerián, was mixing plaster of Paris in a trough while the aunt, in a black dress, prodded the fire with an iron poker, then added some finely ground coal from a pile in the corner.

"Can't stop now! Must keep at it!" Mr. Valerián called out and vomited into the trough.

"I'm glad to hear you say that," said Mr. Mit'ánek, and he laughed when he saw a mirror with a second Mr. Valerián in it, mixing plaster of Paris.

"Valerián," said the aunt, "would you like me to heat you up a nice barley sausage?"

"For the love of God, Auntie, I'm creating!" said Mr. Valerián, and he took a swig from a bottle of bitter red wine.

"We are all creators, because we are all one family," added Mr. Mit'ánek, "but I'm truly impressed." He stood in front of a life-sized portrait and clasped his hands. "What a splendid work of art! The nation will be thrilled!"

"Won't it now!" said the aunt, and she lifted the uncooked barley sausage by its little wooden stick. "But just look at the artist. Look how he's let himself go to seed for the sake of the nation. He never eats a thing, he just drinks, and then there's the damp. See how wrinkled his feet are?"

"Auntie!" roared Mr. Valerián. "Do not piss me off, for the love of God, do not piss me off . . . but . . ." he vomited again into the trough and went on mixing, ". . . can't stop now! Must keep at it!"

The sexton, perched on a rickety stepladder, pushed hard on his screwdriver. A truck pulled up beside the church, then turned into the scrap depot in the courtyard. From his platform on the scaffolding, the stonemason watched as the truck dumped hundreds of red enameled panels into a scrap-metal container. In white lettering, each panel displayed the appellation of a square or a street or a park that had once borne the Generalissimo's name. After the truck left, another truck from the national meat processing works arrived. Onto a pile of scrap paper, it unloaded blood-soaked boxes and wrapping paper with the remnants of tendons, sinews, chunks of flesh, and animal membrane still clinging to them.

As the stonemason held the sandstone eye in place under the statue's graceful eyelid, he noticed his hand was shaking.

He looked around at the high scaffolding enveloping the entire Church of the Most Holy Trinity. It was there so that proletarian hands could restore the building to its former glory.

"It's not easy being a decent communist these days," the stonemason said.

"That's what I like to hear – fighting words," said Mr. Mit'ánek. "But this is quite the surprise. What's it supposed to mean?"

"It's for a competition in honor of Alois Jirásek," said the aunt, as she put the sausage in a frying pan, "and the subject we've chosen is from Jirásek's *Old Czech Legends*. It's Durynk hanging himself from an alder tree because he murdered that little boy. . . . But here's a surprise," the aunt said, wagging her finger, then tapping a mold that stood on a revolving base. "Inside this is a statue of a Lučan warrior," she said in a quiet, singsong voice.

"I'll be a stuffed carp!" said Mr. Mit'ánek, his eyes sparkling. "Is that what you folks have been up to down in this cellar, working to edify the nation?"

Mr. Mit'ánek looked into the eyes of Durynk, who had a noose around his neck, and then he looked over at Mr. Valerián, and saw the same noose hanging from the ceiling above him. He looked at the tunic Mr. Valerián was wearing. "You were your own model for the statue!" Mr. Mit'ánek said, clasping his hands in delight.

Mr. Valerián spat bile into the trough.

"Don't you think I ought to scramble him an egg?" asked the aunt. "Just look at him, how he prostrates himself on the altar of art. That scrawny little butt of his – like an old lady wringing her hands, like two caraway seeds stuck together."

"Will you kindly just shut up, Auntie!" wailed Mr. Valerián, and tears ran down his cheeks.

A pair of men's trousers strode past the window, then someone in a bathing suit, then an entire dog appeared, then some boys ran up, kicked a ball at the wire screen, then flailed away at each other's legs as they clung to the mesh with their fingers.

Mr. Mit'ánek ran into the street. "Snotty-nosed little buggers!" he shouted. "The Master is down there creating something for the sake of your future and what are you doing? You're disturbing him, that's what! I'd love to sic Durynk on you! Or the Lučan warrior!"

But the boys kicked the ball with a thundering blow against the window screen and then volleyed it straight into Mr. Mit'ánek's face. The auxiliary policeman put his hands over his eyes and groped for the door while the aunt hurried out and led him back down into the studio.

"They'll end up juvenile delinquents is what they'll be," said Mr. Mit'ánek, blowing his nose.

"But what's to become of Valerián?" asked the aunt. "Just look at what a wreck his art has made of him! He's shorter by at least four inches. All that creativity has turned him into a hunchback. I know what I'm talking about. I work nights at the National Museum, guarding the stuffed monkeys and apes and those curled up skeletons and all that."

"The best minds in the country are sacrificing themselves for the nation," said Mr. Mit'ánek, blinking a grain of sand out of his eye. "So am I. I'm educating the nation not to jump off moving streetcars."

"Well," said the artist, and he waded into the pile of coal

and vomited, then shook his arms and yelled, "can't stop now! Must keep at it! ... A clear goal ..." and he vomited again, then added, through tears: "... is a cure for fatigue!"

An elderly lady wearing a beret with a little stem on top emerged from Lazarská Street carrying a parcel. She threaded her way through the maze of scaffolding, oblivious to a hand-cart standing there, and when she stepped through some rungs and onto the cart, it tipped, sending her to her knees. She got to her feet again and gazed into the face of St. Jude, while the stonemason, sitting on the statue's lap, was trying to fit it with the new eye. The lady clasped her hands and prayed, her grey curls spilling from under her beret as she looked at the saint's face. The stonemason moved the sandstone eye around until it lined up with the eyebrow but the old lady, in her prayers, was already at one with the superstructure of heaven.

A truck loaded with statues and busts and plaques pulled up in front of the church and turned into the collection de-pot. The man in charge hurried out through the gate and shouted, "Where d'you think you're going with that? That stuff goes straight to the foundry."

He vaulted into the back of the truck, took out a piece of chalk, and wrote a number on the head of each bust. When all the Generalissimo's heads were thus inscribed, he turned, jumped off the truck, and laughed. "Don't even think of try-ing to sell this stuff off as non-ferrous metal."

The truck drove off.

Mr. Valerián filled a stonemason's scoop with white liquid from the mixing trough and ladled it into a hole in the Lučan warrior's head. His aunt anxiously ran her fingers through his hair. "D'you see?" she said. "He's losing his hair, a lot of it!"

"Auntie, for the love of God, do not piss me off!" shouted the artist. "Can't stop now! Must keep going!"

But the Lučan warrior had sprung a leak at the crotch, and white gobs of milky plaster of Paris were dripping onto the concrete floor.

"Auntie," yelled Mr. Valerián, "quick, stick your paws between the warrior's legs!"

"I've just been to church!" she said.

"Shut up! You gave me the last of your money for this plaster of Paris. Quick, or the warrior's going to end up on the floor!"

The aunt wiped her hands on her skirt and then stuck her fingers into the hole in the warrior's crotch.

Mr. Mit'ánek looked into the mirror and was astonished. There were two of everything in the cellar.

"Quick, the warrior's butt has split!" Mr. Valerián shouted, and he went on ladling the plaster of Paris from the trough into the mold.

Mr. Mit'ánek placed his palm between the folds of the warrior's buttocks and felt his hands sealing the leak.

"It's not easy being a decent communist these days," the stonemason said. He sat on the scaffolding beside the mortar trough, swinging his boots close to the old woman's hat as she prayed. He brought his boot to a halt just above her head, and one of his laces grazed her blue beret, but the old lady was still utterly absorbed in the hierarchy of heaven.

The mirrors in the cellar studio stretched from the floor to the ceiling, and Mr. Mit'ánek now understood why the super's wife had given him such a confused report – always two people in the basement, but only one ever left. In the corner, Mr. Mit'ánek saw what first looked like an industrial ironing machine, but on closer inspection it turned out to be an enormous silk-screen press, with rollers almost two yards wide and a frame constructed of solid oak beams and boards.

"Quite the contraption, isn't it?" asked the aunt. "But worse luck, all the jobs we got to do on it were tiny. Valerián had a breakdown over the Christmas and New Year's cards. He was hired to do a card with a photo of a seven-month-old baby boy and they wanted it to look like the baby was sitting on a horse, holding up a sign that said The Kocourek family wish you a Merry Christmas. He went through three cases of cheap wine before he was done. Every half hour he'd toss out everything he'd done so far, but when we worked it out that we'd be getting two thousand crowns for the job, I rescued the photo of the seven-month-old from the garbage, along with the picture of the horse, Valerián stuck his watchmaker's loupe in his eye and copied the boy onto the horse, because it was supposed to look like the real thing."

"And are those things on the wall postage stamps, or are they meant to be matchbox labels?" asked Mr. Mit'ánek.

"No, no," said the aunt. "We've got a commission to do engravings of butterflies and tiny little beetles. This machine runs on an electric motor and makes an awful racket – it weighs eleven hundred kilos – and it's cute to see those huge rollers spitting out a tiny little portrait of a beetle, no bigger than a matchbox label, as you said."

"Shut up, Auntie," shouted Valerián, and he went on ladling the plaster of Paris into the mold.

"The sausage is burning!" yelled the aunt.

"Auntie – don't budge an inch!" he bellowed. At that very moment, the mold split open at the neck, and he quickly poured in the last ladleful and grabbed the warrior by the throat with both hands.

A flatbed truck pulled up in front of the church carrying a huge golden cross wrapped in silk pillowcases and blankets. A crane lowered a sling and tackle over the truck, and two workers carefully wrapped a duvet around the sling. Then the employees of Safina – the company that had gilded the cross – raised it carefully, lifting it by the arms like an invalid, then slipped the sling under it while another worker went to the opposite sidewalk to guide the crane operator with hand signals. The cross was soon suspended in air, about a meter from the stonemason, who sat up and inched backward until he was sitting in the statue's lap with his arms around St. Thaddeus's neck, looking up in alarm at the golden cross, then at the scrap depot with its thousands of unread books, their pages still uncut, then into the scrap-metal container filled with signs that had once indicated all those Prague squares and streets and parks named after the Generalissimo.

"It's enough to make you puke," he said quietly.

The boys kicked the ball down the cul de sac.

"Marty!" called Mr. Valerián. "Marty, come down here a minute."

One of the boys knelt down and peered into the basement window. "What is it, Mr. Valerián?" he said, out of breath.

"Come down here, Marty. I'm dying for a smoke. My cigarettes are on the table. Take one and stick it in my mouth. As you can see, we're all a bit immobilized," he said, indicating the strange tableau with his chin.

The door opened and a breathless boy hurried into the cellar, his socks down around his ankles.

"Over there on the table.... Not there? Then they're probably in my pants pocket," said Mr. Valerián, pointing with his chin.

The boy moved under the bright lightbulb and slipped his hand into the artist's pocket.

"Marty!" shrieked a woman's voice. Mrs. Karásková was squatting down at the window and peering in, her eyes crazed with worry at the sight of her beloved little boy groping about in Mr. Valerián's pants.

"God knows I'd just as soon blow this church to smithereens," said the sexton. He removed the first plaque, placed it in a laundry hamper, and shook his hands to get the circulation going again in his fingers. "I'm sick and tired of these cults."

The stonemason now barely paid any attention when another truck drove into the depot. He watched idly as they tossed basketfuls of letters onto the pile of scrap paper, covering the bloodstained paper and boxes from the meat-processing plant. Nor was he surprised to learn that there were seven hundred kilos of letters, all written by Prague school children in response to an essay contest, sponsored by the radio, on the theme: How can we make our country ever more beautiful?

Then the old lady in the beret walked into the depot, put her little bundle on the scales, the manager weighed it, then tossed it onto the pile, and said: "That's five kilos. Here's one crown."

"One crown?" complained the old lady. "There were letters in that bundle from my lovers!"

"Lady, I'm sorry, but this ain't no auction house. I don't care if Rudolph Valentino wrote you those letters, you get exactly the same: twenty hellers a kilo, one crown for five kilos. *Eine krone!*" he shouted, but the old lady was already up to her waist in scrap paper, ploughing her way through the bloody papers and animal membranes, whimpering in pain, until at last she waded out of the pile with her bundle, her hands smeared with blood. She untied it and held something up.

"These, I'll have you know, are letters written to me by a lieutenant in the lancers, and this is one from someone who robbed a cash box just for my sake and ended up in Spandau Prison. And here ..."

"Look, lady," the manager said, "this here's a scrap-paper depot, but you've made your point. Here's five crowns, from my own pocket. Now clear out!" He took a step forward, kicked the air, then wiped his forehead.

"The mirrors don't lie," said Mr. Mit'ánek.

"You've seen *It Happened in Broad Daylight*, haven't you?" the mother shrieked. "If that isn't enough for you, what is?" She shook the wire mesh, unaware that as she crouched down, the better to see into the cellar, she had spread her legs wide apart. Her son, Marty, ran out of the basement.

"Mrs. Karásková, please. I'm a volunteer police officer," Mr. Mit'ánek said. "Don't make a public issue out of this."

But Mrs. Karásková whacked the child, and the sound of his wailing faded in the distance. The boys resumed their game, kicking the ball against the screen and practicing the Wall Pass.

"Don't you think all this art has made Valerián's ears stick out?" asked the aunt. "They're kind of like parchment, like he was at death's door. Even his nose is looking a little blue . . ."

"For the love of God, Auntie!" shouted Mr. Valerián. "I could strangle you, just like this," and he cocked his chin toward the mold containing the Slavic warrior.

"I might be able to persuade the local council to send you to a holiday camp, free of charge," said Mr. Miťánek. "I have a lot of clout with them," and he laughed at the thought that one day, perhaps, when they wrote about the artist who had once worked in a cellar on a cul de sac, his own name might figure in the story, too.

"I'm fine, but if you could just . . ." Mr. Valerián said, and he turned to vomit over his shoulder, ". . . if you could just help me carry that painting to the competition."

The old lady left the depot bent over like a broken bush, carrying her letters. She walked over to St. Thaddeus and held up a set of photos for the saint to see, utterly unconcerned that the stonemason sitting on the scaffolding beside his mortar trough could see them as well.

"My dear, sweet Thaddeus, d'you see this? This one was me, Cleo, the dancer, and here's a picture from Leipzig, when our tigers escaped. I danced with them in a cage. They got out and posed in front of this monument, all eight of them, making a tableau because they thought it was part of the act. And here's one of them chasing after a streetcar, and people were passing out. And here's where they turned a hose on them, and the tigers gamboled about in the water because they thought it was part of the act, too, and they had to shoot them in the end. Here's a picture of the police posing with the dead tigers, and here's one when their trainer showed up, and when she saw her darling animals lying there dead, she shot herself too.... My dear, sweet Thaddeus, can you still see Cleo the dancer locked up inside me?"

Mr. Valerián, the artist, and Mr. Mit'ánek, the auxiliary policeman, stood in front of a large wrought-iron gate decorated with gilded lilies. A footpath of golden sand wound its way under some elm trees and through a pleasure garden with a palace at the end of it. They walked up the path and came to a porter's lodge in front of the palace. Straddling a chair was a porter, staring intently at the red carpet that emerged like a giant tongue from the palace entrance. A man walked out onto the carpet, his arms spread wide, his face ashen, making gagging noises. The porter stood up, grabbed a bucket from under a box hedge, held it under the gentleman's chin, dropped the handle over his neck, and, while the man was throwing up, the porter wiped flecks of vomit from his chest. When the man finished vomiting, he walked away, hiccupping and whimpering softly to himself, his eyes wet with tears. He wobbled along the pathway, past Mr. Mit'ánek and Mr. Valerián, barely able to navigate his way out through the ornate gateway.

"The jury must be having some kind of banquet," said Mr. Mit'ánek, rubbing his hands.

"So, what have you got for us?" asked the porter, as he put the bucket and the rag back behind the box hedge.

"It's for the Jirásek competition," Mr. Miťánek said, pointing to the large framed picture covered with a sheet.

"You'll want the second floor then. The ground floor is already filled up – can you guess with what?" asked the porter, then he turned away and shouted, "Vašek! Don't make me take my belt off!"

"Portraits of Jan Kozina at the gallows?" asked Mr. Valerián.

"Is that what you're bringing us? A Kozina?" asked the porter. He turned and made as though he were getting ready to undo his belt. "Vašek, stop throwing sand in Ferda's eyes or I'll give you a thrashing."

"A Kozina," said Mr. Valerián.

"Good thinking," said the porter. "Every painter thought the others would do Kozina, so we only have twenty-five of those, but hang onto your hat," the porter laughed. "Durynk, the traitor and murderer Durynk? As of today, they've brought in – and I don't want to lie to you," he said, leaning into the porter's booth, "they've brought in ninety-six Durynks."

"Good thing I'm submitting a Kozina," Mr. Valerián said, shuddering.

The stonemason hopped down from his perch, the sexton looked at his watch, then both entered the bell tower and started up the winding staircase.

"Are they going to use dynamite?" asked the stonemason.

"No, and they're not even using ekrasite," the sexton said, "they're using donorite." Then he turned and hurried up the corkscrew stairway. Through the tower windows, they could see that they were now higher than the surrounding rooftops. When they reached the level where the bell hung, they looked through the gothic window frames and out over the city. Across the river stood a gigantic statue crosshatched with scaffolding.

"A German company offered to dismantle it with a special cutting tool, but they didn't want cash for it, they wanted a supply of Carlsbad clay to make fine china. Instead, we offered to buy their saw outright, but the Germans said the saw was special and not for sale. So the job went to a Swiss company," the sexton said, sitting down on the gothic windowsill and placing a telescope in his lap. The breeze made waves in his hair. "They drilled sixteen hundred holes altogether. When the engineer gives the signal, they'll throw the switch and the whole statue will come apart, piece by piece."

"Right," said the stonemason, his voice failing him. He stood with his legs braced, his white trouser legs and jacket flapping in the breeze. He leaned forward, propped his arms against the sandstone window frame, and stared across the city at the opposite river bank. The palms of his hands were dry.

"Seven people all told were killed in the building of it," the sexton went on. "The first to die was the sculptor who designed it, and the last was a worker's mate who came to work one Monday morning three sheets to the breeze and he put his foot through a board six levels up and fell head first off the scaffolding and smashed his skull on the Generalissimo's little finger."

Mr. Valerián and Mr. Mit'ánek entered the palace and followed the red carpet up the staircase, each carrying one end of the picture, so, from the side, they looked like the rectangular pig little children draw on walls. At the top of the stairs, they propped the painting up against the gilded wainscoting. "Maybe the porter was bullshitting," said Mr. Mit'ánek.

Mr. Valerián entered the large salon on the second floor and, as if in a trance, walked past the paintings leaning against the wall. It was as though he were walking in and out of one mirror after another, one painting after another, as if he himself were Durynk. Ninety-six times he walked in and out of the same picture, until he reemerged into the hall under golden chandeliers and golden balustrades.

"He wasn't bullshitting," said Mr. Mit'ánek.

Mr. Valerián took hold of his painting and carried it roughly down the corridor and into the washroom, where he locked himself inside one of the cubicles. As Mr Mit'ánek stood at a urinal, pretending to relieve himself in case anyone walked in, he heard a strange sound. At first he thought Mr. Valerián must be having an attack of diarrhea, but then he recognized it as the sound of ripping canvas. The cubicle door opened, and Mr. Valerián emerged without the picture. He handed a small piece of canvas to Mr. Mit'ánek.

"A souvenir, from me," he said with a forced laugh.

The strip showed the eyes of the wretched Durynk cut from the canvas with a knife, like eyes seen through a peephole in a door. Mr. Mit'ánek realized that the look in Mr. Valerián's eyes was exactly the same, a look he hadn't had back in the studio, but did now.

Mr. Valerián began to gag and turn pale. He ran down the red carpet, his arms wide, and staggered out into the sunlight. He saw the porter's dark silhouette and then the large bucket looming in front of him and he threw up into it, feeling the metallic handle slip over his head and press against the nape of his neck. He felt like a dray horse, when the driver slips on a feedbag filled with oats.

"So you tried to bluff me," the porter said sympathetically, wiping Mr. Valerián's chest with a rag. "You submitted a Durynk, too, didn't you?"

Mr. Valerián nodded, and tears rolled down his cheeks. Along the sand-strewn path two workers from a delivery service approached; in a strap sling, they carried a sandstone statue of a warrior dressed in animal skins brandishing a stone axe. They hurried up the stairs with the statue, their legs scissoring as they went, and when Mr. Valerián looked at them, his stomach began to heave again but he had nothing left to bring up, so he bellowed into the bucket as though he were blowing on a French horn. The porter watched the statue disappear up the stairs and then gave a whistle.

"Uh oh, you did a warrior statue too. Go on, admit it. You did, didn't you?" The porter slapped Mr. Valerián on the back.

"How many warriors have you delivered so far today?" the porter shouted into the foyer.

"This is the eleventh," one of the men shouted back.

"That's quite a helping," said the porter, and he carefully removed the bucket from Mr. Valerián's neck, wiped his shirt front, and set the bucket down by the box hedge.... "Vašek! My belt's coming off! Stop throwing sand in Ferda's eyes."

"Out of curiosity, how many of those warriors have they brought in ... I mean in total?" asked Mr. Miťánek.

"A hundred and ten," said the porter. "Which is why I say,

enough with the art already. This here's the thing," and he held up a little book, shaking it at them. "Nobody can trump Einstein! A great read, this, like a whodunit. So enough with the art already. Einstein predicted everything. He exposed all the old fantasies, completely trashed them. He said there was dark matter in the universe and sure enough, there was ... Vašek! I'm taking my belt off!" The porter made to remove his belt, but then went on excitedly: "Einstein figured the earth wasn't perfectly round, and sure enough, it wasn't. He figured that the speed of light in a vacuum is independent of the speed of the light source.... Vašek! ... It's like when a swallow dips down and touches the surface of the water with its wing. Einstein established the outer limits of speed, saying that no signal can travel faster than light, but ... Vašek, that's the goddamned limit!" ... and in a sudden rage, the porter yanked off his belt and plunged into the bushes, bent a little boy across his knee, and thrashed him, while a second little boy sat sobbing his eyes out.

The stonemason cringed.

"Inside, the entire statue is made of solid concrete, reinforced with special underground buttresses that reach all the way across to the Sparta football stadium," the sexton said. "They reckon the demolition will take thirty days."

"Right," the stonemason said, coughing nervously.

"I wonder why they don't just leave all those Prague statues standing," said the sexton, extending his telescope, then looking at his watch. "Think of all the statuary there'd be in Prague now, almost a thousand years' worth! If they didn't keep tearing them down, there'd be so many statues in Prague, you'd never have to fall on your face walking home drunk – there'd always be an arm of marble or sandstone to lean on."

The porter did up his belt and took a deep breath. "So let's say the swallow touches the water with its wingtips," he continued, "and the ripples start to spread out across the water, but the speed of the ripples has nothing to do with how fast the swallow is flying. See what I'm saying?" he said to Mr. Mit'ánek.

"I see," said Mr. Mit'ánek, and he looked at the boy, who was just standing there awkwardly. "You should tell that to Mr. Valerián here. He's the artist. I'm just an auxiliary cop. What's wrong with the lad's shoulder?"

"Oh that? It's nothing," the porter said dismissively. "He was in his mother's body longer than he should have been, so they had to break a bone or two to get him out. They broke his shoulder. When he's seven, they'll break it again and fix it for good. But back to this Einstein, d'you see what I'm getting at? Compared to this Jirásek competition?"

"I see," said Mr. Valerián. "Can't stop now, though. Must keep at it."

"Right," said the porter. He looked toward the bright red carpet, then picked up the bucket and the rag from beside the box hedge. "Another Lučan warrior!" he shouted, and hurried to meet the new arrival, holding out the bucket.

Mr. Valerián threw up briefly onto the lawn, then he and Mr. Mit'ánek walked quickly down the pathway, through the pleasure garden, past two artists who were just arriving, each carrying a canvas wrapped in sheets.

A flash of light, and a dark cloud of smoke erupted from the construction enveloping the statue, followed by an enormous thud. A kind of force ripped through it, the first level lifted slightly off the ground and the pipes whirled into the air like lances, spinning higher and higher, and when the force began to dissipate, they hung suspended for an instant, then rained down on the ground around the statue, creating a thicket of lance-like branches. Half the scaffolding was completely blown away, the other half separated from the statue but remained upright, tottering unsteadily like a ski jump on the verge of collapse. The statue now stood exposed, apparently stronger, more massive than ever, but tilted forward as though it were about to go crashing down on the city below. The wall of air the explosion had set in motion rushed across the city rooftops, causing the church bell to resonate faintly and the stonemason's coveralls to flap like a flag in the wind.

"Someone's going to be in deep trouble," said the sexton. "Everything just kind of held together. As far as I can see," he added, putting down his telescope, "all that came off the old man was an eye, the epaulets, and a knee, the same as what's missing from the statue you're working on."

The stonemason leaned out the window and looked down at the gilded cross being gradually hauled upward, suspended in a sling from the Safina National Enterprise crane. He knew that scaffolders' hands had put up the seven-story structure around the Generalissimo's statue, that he and other workers had drilled those holes with pneumatic drills at sixteen hundred different points, each marked with a cross, and, as the work had proceeded, that he had personally drilled holes, first in both the Generalissimo's eyes, and then in a spot in the stone where the Generalissimo's heart would have been: it felt as if he were drilling a hole into his own heart because he, the stonemason, loved the Generalissimo, had invested his hopes in him, had lived his life through him, and now he'd not only had to participate in the destruction of his enormous monument, but he'd also had to listen to exhortations to wipe the Generalissimo's picture from his heart, a picture so dear to him he felt he couldn't go on living without it.

He thought about the other picture that was eating away at him at night, for he now realized that those same scaffolders were today standing on each others' shoulders like a troupe of acrobats, passing pipes and planks from hand to hand until they'd enveloped the entire Church of the Most Holy Trinity, where he was cementing, to a Catholic statue eroded by weather and time, a new sandstone knee and an eye he'd brought with him in his satchel that morning, along with some salami and a bun. It was all so that, through the restoration of this particular Catholic church, the Church itself could resound once more in its original pomp and splendor.

The summer this year was a hot one. Mr. Valerián and Mr. Mit'ánek felt cooler as soon as they descended into the studio.

"It's like going to the patent office and claiming I'd invented the bicycle," said Mr. Valerián, standing in front of the white-plaster statue of the warrior brandishing his plaster-of-Paris stone axe.

"Still," said Mr. Mit'ánek, "it's a thing of beauty."

Mr. Valerián took a swig from the bottle of cheap red wine, then picked up a hatchet and with a single blow lopped off the warrior's hand, stone axe and all, then he smashed the head and sliced the statue in half at the waist. He stared into the mirrors for a long time, drinking the bitter red wine and talking, throwing up a little at the end of every sentence.

"The mirrors betrayed me," he said, and he smashed them with his axe, shattering himself, shattering his own image.

"I can see you don't believe in cheap imitations," shouted Mr. Mit'ánek. "And you probably don't believe that as an auxiliary policeman, I can sit down this evening and write all this up, do you?"

Mr. Mit'ánek shook his finger and followed Mr. Valerián around as Mr. Valerián carried the warrior, piece by piece, to the trash bin. The last to go in were the legs, but the lid wouldn't shut and the warrior's ankles and feet protruded from the bin. The aunt came around the corner of the alley, carrying soup in an aluminum pot and a casserole tied up in a bundle. "Don't you think Mr. Valerián might have water on the brain?" she said.

"Oh, shut up, Auntie," said Mr. Valerián. He went back into the cellar, curling up in a ball on the pile of coal dust, muttering to himself: "Can't stop now! Must keep going . . . ," and he began to sob like a little child.

"Working men," said the stonemason quietly. "It's all been a terrible con."

He leaned out the window and looked down into the scrap depot, thinking that if he had any backbone at all, he would jump out of this bell tower as if from a high diving board, taking a good run at it, with his head up so the workers on the scaffolding down below would see that it was deliberate, that it wasn't an accident, and he'd spread his arms in a swan dive, plummet into the courtyard, and smash himself to pieces on the pile of scrap metal, on the plaques that had marked all those streets and avenues and squares and parks named after the Generalissimo, and if he were lucky, he'd plunge all the way through to the pile of scrap paper and die surrounded by seven hundred kilograms of letters sent by the children of Prague with suggestions about how to make the country an ever more beautiful place.

The summer this year was a hot one. Boys bounced soccer balls off the walls, practicing the Czech Wall Pass.

Breaking Through the Drum

I never felt better than when I was tearing the stubs off people's tickets and showing them to their seats. In primary school, I loved to make seating plans for the teacher. Then during the war, a weird thing happened to me. A kind of ticket taker's demon lit on my back and right in the middle of the newsreel, when the voice announced that eighty-eight enemy aircraft had been shot down over Dortmund and only one German plane had gone missing, the perverse little imp whispered something in my ear, and I said in a loud voice: "Aw shucks, it's bound to turn up again." My voice sounded like it belonged to somebody else, so I turned up the house lights and ordered the person who'd said it to come forward. The other ushers and I walked through the audience, but no one confessed and so, invoking our official powers, and we actually had such powers, I declared that the entire program, including the feature film, was hereby cancelled, the tickets were null and void and, as punishment, everyone had to go home without a refund.

But I didn't become an honest-to-goodness ticket taker

until later, when I was working the aisles at the Time Cinema. That's where I got the chance to be a kind of supervisor as well. I didn't just show people to their seats, I also made sure no one tried to sit through the movie twice. For the first time I was really enjoying myself, and I would feel let down at the end of the shift if I hadn't been able to grab a patron by the scruff just as he was settling in to watch the movie all over again, in other words, as he was about to defraud the Time Cinema. I'd only have to look at people, and they'd know I was in charge. At intermission, I'd pull the curtains back and open the windows to air the place while the customers who'd seen the complete show were filing out. I'd stand with my arm behind my back, holding the door open for them, while the audience for the next showing was lining up outside, and when the last departing customer had shown his heels I'd open the swinging doors again and tear the first tickets of the new arrivals, at the same time keeping an eagle eye out for anyone still in his seat who'd already seen part of the show, making careful note of when his ticket expired. I also couldn't stand it when young people talked during the newsreel, because I felt responsible for each showing and I'd lean over and say loudly: "Hush, or they'll lock us all up!" and my voice was firm enough to command silence; but I still wasn't persuaded, so I'd stand down by the front row and scan their faces to see if they were really watching the screen or not, and I would usher other patrons to their seats and sometimes ask a whole row to shift over so I could seat a customer precisely where I wanted him to fit my ideal seating plan. I also bought an atomizer with my own money and during intermission I'd spray a solution of aromatic oil into the air. And so I became a bona fide ticket taker for the simple reason that I felt in charge. That was also why I got promoted and became an usher in first-class theatres, concert venues, and public lecture halls.

I applied the same method at home with my family. The only person I was really close to was my brother-in-law, who stamped the passports of people traveling abroad. When we had time on our hands we'd go to restaurants where, just for fun, I'd invent seating plans. I'd tell my brother-in-law which customers belonged and which ones I'd toss out, who I'd seat where, and who I'd show the door when they'd had too much to drink or if they'd gotten tipsy somewhere else and just come in for a final round or to make trouble. My brother-in-law would sit there watching the customers arrive and he'd say quietly: "His passport I'd stamp, and his I would not." My brother-in-law classified people according to whether or not he'd let them leave the country. And although after they'd left it wasn't really his concern any more, he felt responsible for people's trips abroad, and was always wondering, right down to the wire, whether he'd done the right thing in stamping someone's passport or not. Twice, a plane took off while he was still on board, and he'd been taken into custody at the other end, once in Vienna and once in Paris. Then again, my brother-in-law had his own perverse little imp, and it befuddled him several times, to the point where he'd stamp the passport of someone he was sure was kosher only to find out later that the guy had defected, while someone he was certain was trying to emigrate would surprise everyone by coming back.

Anyway, the day before yesterday I was ushering at the

Ledeburg Terraces where they were putting on a tragedy about a black guy by the name of Othello who ends up murdering his wife in her own bed. It wasn't just paying customers who watched it; people living in the apartments overlooking the gardens could watch through their open windows, free of charge. I went to the apartments so I could at least sell them standing-room tickets, but they locked the gate on me. I fetched a ladder, but as I was climbing over the wall I fell and landed on my hands, practically wrenching my arms out of their sockets, and when I looked up the gate was open again, but while I was fetching the ladder someone slammed it back shut. I heard the key turning in the lock so I knocked to be let in, because I'd dropped my book of tickets on the other side. I couldn't get it back, and to avoid being made fun of, I paid for all fifty standing-room tickets out of my own pocket, which earned me a pat on the back. At the end of the play, just when the noble Moor was strangling his wife, Desdemona, someone began strangling a woman on the second floor of the apartment building, and in the struggle the woman got shoved out the window just as the Moor was finishing off Desdemona, and people in the audience stood up because they thought they were seeing things, and I tried to calm them down but couldn't.... So I went back and, by the powers vested in me, I climbed the ladder, put my fingers to my lips and like a proper usher, I shushed the people standing around the woman in the courtyard. But she was lying on the ground with a broken leg, howling in pain, and I looked down into the courtyard and then back at the Ledeburg Terraces, and I realized that the wounded woman was none of my business, that my main concern was to make sure the play finished without interruption. When it was finally over, I climbed down, the audience applauded, the fellow who played the Moor, wet with his own tears, stood there receiving the applause like a dead man. Immediately afterward, we carried the woman from the small courtyard to an ambulance, and for the first time in my life I felt as if I'd taken cotton plugs out of my ears. I could hear the final applause rising from the Ledeburg Terraces and the tears and moans of the husband and that woman, and I heard all of it at the same time, yet each sound was separate too. I could hear it all clearly: the creaking of the seats being folded up, the squeal of hinges as the tenants opened their windows and leaned out, the conversations on either side of the wall, and everything suddenly seemed so bizarre I thought my ticket taker's demon must have come back to play with my mind.

And the strange state continued into yesterday, when I worked a string-quartet concert, tearing tickets and ushering customers to their seats. A very select audience goes to hear a string quartet: preoccupied people with careworn, melancholy faces, including young girls you just know will go home in the end with a bun in the oven because a proper string quartet can make you defenseless. When the quartet began to play, I went to the top of the stairs at the back of the Ledeburg Terraces and sat beside the statues on the sandstone wall, and I put one leg across my knee and rested my chin in my hand, following the battle of the instruments – because I have always felt that a real string quartet is like a feud, or a bar brawl, or a fistfight in the town square, a life-and-death struggle, and over the years, I've learned to see stories and events in a string quartet to amuse myself, while

I'm watching the audience sitting there in rows to make sure no one has passed out or is causing a disturbance. Yesterday, just as the quartet was coming to the climax and the cello seemed to be winning hands down, the second violin ripped into him and tore him to shreds. It looked like the first violin might come out on top because it was holding back on the sidelines, the way it is when three people are in a fight and the fourth one stands aside, laughing, and you could see it in the listeners, because most of them seemed diminished – cowed and bent, holding their heads in their hands, as though they were nursing a toothache. Just then, a little fellow in the front row stood up and edged his way backward among the chairs. I knew from experience that he was from out of town and worried about missing the last bus or the last train home, and I could see that he was backing straight toward a fish pond filled with water lilies, and if he continued, he'd trip on the low stone edging around the pond and fall backward into the water and cause a commotion. I knew I had to act quickly and come down from my sandstone perch and catch him by the shoulders at the last moment and then gently guide him to the exit. But my private demon whispered in my ear: don't do anything, wait and see what happens. I looked up, and the drone of an airplane with colored lights on its wingtips joined in with the music of the quartet, and along with it I heard the clang of a trolley and it all merged into a kind of symphony, and I looked back down and saw that everything was happening as it should: the little man was only a few feet from the pool, the rest of the audience seemed dead, as though a line from yesterday's play – "Behold what the scythe has laid low!" – applied to them. Then the man's heels caught on the stones, and he tumbled backward, his little body mirrored in the pool, and for an instant, he curled up like a child in the womb, like the drawings in my *Handbook of Home Medicine*, and then a splash, and he went under and came up soaking wet and draped with lily pads, two buds resting on his shoulders like the pips on a general's epaulets, and as he stood there up to his waist in water he unbuttoned his jacket and a tiny goldfish popped out of his vest, and the patrons in the rows nearest the pool backed away, some running up the stairs in my direction to distance themselves from the embarrassment, so no one would think it was them who'd brought the little man to the concert or that they might be related ... and I heard the quartet drifting apart, and the cello, which was probably destined to lose the battle, deliberately contributing to the general cacophony; then the ushers pulled the man out of the pond, and someone laughed, but nothing upset me, not even when two of the musicians stopped playing altogether, and the first violinist, deprived of his triumph, ran down the narrow aisle between the rows of seats, arriving just as the ushers were dragging the little man out of the water by his trousers and, as they were pulling his trousers back up, the violinist whacked the little man with his bow, then again, then a third time, with a smack that sounded like a slab of meat slapping against a barn door, and I was on tenterhooks, trembling at the beauty, the utter beauty of it all, and several patrons were pounding their fists against the back wall until the stucco cracked loose, and others were scratching at it with their fingernails as though trying to climb out, but for me, everything meshed, everything blended with everything else, and my heart howled with pleasure. "I had no intention of disturbing you," the little man said. "I have a train to catch." Afterward, I went home dumbstruck by everything that had happened, and when I unlocked the door, the jingle of the key was like music, and I was even at peace with the fact that my daughter hadn't come home yet.

Today, since the early morning, I stood on a street corner, amazed. The streetcars and human conversation, each thing responded to the other, like good footballers passing the ball. A flashy young man, whose passport my brother never would have stamped, was standing beside me holding under his arm a packet of newspapers or something tied with binder twine. Then a car ran over the curb onto the sidewalk and back down again, and two cops looking on just laughed, and the young man came up to them and said, "Didn't you see that car?" And the cops replied, "Anything wrong with that?" The young man said, "Anything wrong with that? I'll show you what's wrong with that!" and he tore the cover off his packet and shook a sheaf of funeral notices in their faces, saying, "My mother was hit by a car that ran over the curb like that!" He held up the funeral notices with both hands, the way a priest holds up the monstrance during the holy sacrament, and it all fit together for me, even the sound of tearing paper, everything harmonized, even this morning when I stood by my daughter's bedside, watching her sleep, and her nightdress had slipped up to reveal a nicely shaped calf, and any other time I'd have raised the roof and demanded to know where she'd been last night. But today, I could only gaze at her, moved by her beauty, and I walked out of her room without a sound, past my wife who was white with fear that I'd make a scene. I caressed the back of her hand, and she snatched it away as though I'd bitten her, and a boy was skipping down our street on one foot, shouting to anyone who'd listen: "My mum and dad are getting married!" I wasn't scandalized in the least, I did the opposite of what I'd have done as a proper ticket taker and supervisor, I patted the young lad's head and then looked at my hand and felt the pleasure the gesture had given me; and then I came across a hearse with a coffin inside, then another with two, and a bit further on, a third carrying three coffins, and I said to myself, you'd better take a side street, because God knows what kind of evil omen you'll come across next, and as I was tying my shoelaces, someone rolled up a storefront shutter with a terrible clatter, and I jumped up and ran across the street and found myself standing in front of the Prague Municipal Funeral Service, and on each floor there were coffins in various stages of manufacture, and on the ground floor, on the other side of the shutter, the coffins were stacked neatly like in a warehouse full of black shoes. Any other time I'd have been knocked for a loop, but today I just smiled. A Russian Tupolev flew over the city, and everything came together in a grand symphony. I felt like I was becoming a rotten ticket taker, a rotten supervisor, and was turning into someone else, as though someone had taken the plugs not just out of my ears but out of my soul as well, or taken the blinders off my eyes, as though I'd been a cab driver's nag until now, and on my way home for lunch, I bought a box of pastries and a panel truck nosed up alongside me, and a guy leaned out and asked where the pub called U Pudilů was. I said, "They used to call it that, my friend, but now it's got a sign that says U Kroftů, but everyone calls it U Marků." And the driver was thrilled and pounded his fist on the door like it was the kettle drum in a symphony, like in Beethoven's Fifth, and he said, "Glad to know that, 'cause I've been around this block four times, but you know what?" and he jumped out of his cab and said, "Let me show you something, a kid who's been torn to shreds." And he went around to the back of the truck, opened the doors, and there was an ordinary-looking coffin. So I said, "My friend, I've got a vivid imagination, and I can see him right here" – and I tapped my forehead with my finger – "not only worse than he actually is, but far worse than he could ever be. That's the size of it!" And I went home and my wife and daughter were white with fear, they kept spilling their soup on the tablecloth, dropping pieces of meat on the floor, but in my mind, everything was as it should be, so I just smiled, which frightened them more than if I'd started shouting and threatening to beat them, and they got even more upset when I brought out the box of pastries and said, "Go ahead, open it up," and my daughter wrung her hands and couldn't bring herself to do it, because she must have thought I'd bought her baby clothes, and my wife broke her fingernails trying to undo the knots and then she cut the string and I had to open the lid myself.... Inside were cakes and cream puffs, and I held the box out, but my wife and daughter backed up against the wall and if they could have, they'd have retreated right through the wall into the neighbors' apartment, and I grew serious and began to sweat and took a cream puff out of the box and put it in my daughter's hand, then I did the same for my wife, and they just stood there, holding the pastries I'd bought them, something I'd never done before, each holding a cream puff they couldn't bring themselves to taste.... "Go on, try them, I bought them for you," I said, and I took one myself and ate it, and they lifted the pastries to their mouths and finally took a nibble, but they couldn't even swallow that tiny morsel, and I could hear that what I'd seen this morning in the street and now here at home was part and parcel with the *Symphonie Pathétique*, which I'd be hearing for the thirty-seventh time that evening as a ticket taker, a symphony I'd have to set up for this afternoon, putting out folding chairs and making sure the cleaning ladies dusted the seats properly. My wife and daughter hung their heads, staring at the carpet, and I couldn't see their eyes because their hair hid their faces and almost touched the cream puffs they held trembling in their fingers. That's what you get for wanting to impose order on everything, I thought, or would have, if my old way of thinking hadn't been blocked.

It's not easy to be a good ticket taker in the Waldstein Gardens. There's a lot of dispute over whose bailiwick it is, because a high wall separates the Waldstein Gardens from the St. Thomas brewery next door, and although it's difficult to climb over, the wall doesn't block the sounds of music or conversation. It's a real test of a good supervisor's nerves when the Prague Municipal Symphony Orchestra, under the baton of Doctor Smetáček, plays the same evening as Mr. Polata's Šumava Regional Brass Band on the other side of the wall. It always leads to conflict, because each side thinks the other is interfering with its music. And since I'd torn tickets and ushered exclusively for these elite performances in the Waldstein

Gardens, I couldn't stand the beer gardens at St. Thomas's, and the very sound of a brass band would turn my stomach. My brother-in-law was different and although he stamped passports for a living, he was a simple man who loved his beer and other worldly pleasures. So Waldstein was right to have had such a high wall built, as though he'd known all along that the Czech nation would be divided. I was not divided, however: I stood firmly on the side of symphonic music, and often, during a concert, I found myself daydreaming about how I'd put a ladder against the wall, climb over it, and pound all the patrons and their brass band into unconsciousness. I harbored such high-minded notions until now, when I felt in my bones that I'd reversed the course of my thinking and that today something was bound to happen. When the conductor came out and tapped his baton on his music stand and the audience fell silent, you could hear Mr. Polata's brass band playing a clamorous polka. The musicians stared painfully into the whispering crowns of the ancient trees. After that, there was nothing to do but take Mr. Polata's music on, so now it was the Prague Municipal Symphony Orchestra's turn to start poking its nose into the flowering garden of the St. Thomas brewery. The *Symphonie Pathétique* began, and the conductor directed it like a high priest, but as for me, I heard Mr. Polata's brass band not as an enemy but an ally, and the brass band's music blended with the *Symphonie Pathétique* as though they'd been written by the same composer ... and for the first time, I imagined that there were people on the other side of the wall, not just a bunch of barbarians, but people living by their own lights, with beer and brass-band music, and they were probably just as fond of that as I was of the Prague Municipal Symphony

Orchestra, so it wasn't just them getting in our way, the inter-
ference was mutual, and I heard that old chestnut, Wald-
teufel's *Skater's Waltz*, floating over the wall and blowing a kiss
to the *Pathétique* and no one could stop it from happening, or
if so, it would mean stopping one to the detriment of the
other, or, like me, you could learn to listen to everything at
once, though to do that, you needed patience. Usually I stood
leaning against the broad trunk of a tree, but today I gradually
moved into the shadows under a large branch, until I reached
the wall, where I bumped into a small man pounding the wall
with his fist. Then he put his ear to it, and I put my ear to it
too, and I could hear the scraping of brogues and oxfords on
the brewery's sandy dance floor and the dancers' heavy
breathing and their conversations, and over it all a great tree
of brass-band music opened out. I felt a powerful urge now, as
never before, to see what was happening on the other side of
the wall. So overwhelming was the urge that it led me to remember that there were ladders in the Waldstein's aviary, so I
opened the screen door to the place where they had once
raised vultures and eagles. The mesh ceiling wasn't there anymore, but I saw three ladders leaning against the wall and
climbed quietly up one with the Adagio splashing at my back,
and up where I was heading, one rung at a time, there was
more light and more music as well. . . . The trees were resting
their branches on the top of the wall, but I pushed them out of
the way and looked down on the other side, and though I
could easily have just walked into the brewery, today was different, today I saw it through the *Symphonie Pathétique* and I
was going to look down at the other half of my new self,
whence like a breeze, the tones of the brass instruments were

wafting upward along with the aroma of beer and the fragrance of women … one more rung and there it was, just, it seemed to me, as it had been with the string quartet. Through the branches and between the leaves, I saw, in the yellow glow, an array of square tablecloths with glasses of beer on them, I saw the square dance floor and the people dressed in black and white and busty women swirling in circles, one hand hanging free, the other resting lightly on the napes of their partners' necks as they spun around, their faces flushed, while the men held them round the waist or placed their faces against their cheeks as if the dancers were drinking in one another's breath … and then I saw a beautiful woman standing in the middle of the garden surrounded by four men who might have been tailors, using a tape measure to measure her waist and her bust, then each breast separately, as if they were judges in a contest to choose the queen of the bounteous bosom, and one of the men drew white lines on her body with tailor's chalk, lines of classic beauty, covering her black evening dress and tracing the shape of what lay beneath, those classic arcs and intersections and who knows what else, and I heard everything that was going on here dissolved in the music that came from behind, from across the wall. I glanced back for a moment to see the audience in the Waldstein Gardens holding their cheeks and their chins, for the music had so undone them they had to support their heads in their hands, whereas on this side the dancers, men and women, were moved to cheer ecstatically in response to the joy that flowed from Mr. Polata's music … and waitresses walked among them, their backs arched, carrying a bouquet of five brimming beer glasses in each hand, moving from table to table, marking the beer mats with pencil strokes. Then the *Skater's Waltz* ended; the musicians blew the spittle out of their instruments, while the women let their partners hold on to them and lead them back to their tables, their hands still curled gently around the mens' necks, and now they were playing the finale of the *Symphonie Pathétique*, the Adagio lamentoso, and some of the men in the beer garden walked over to the wall and shouted over into the Waldstein Gardens: "To hell with your Beethoven! Goddamned Mozart! Killjoys!" The little man had climbed up through the aviary and appeared on the wall beside me, tugging my sleeve and saying, "Aren't you in charge here? Why don't you do something?" But I had just seen my brother-in-law sitting in the beer garden at a table with two plates on it, next to the entrance where they were taking admission, and my brother-in-law was no doubt amusing himself by picking the dancers he'd let travel abroad and those he wouldn't. But then I saw it! Surrounding the beer garden on three sides was a monastery that was now an old folks' home for women, and in every window on the second and third floor I could see the bright eyes of these old women staring down in the same direction, at the queen of the bounteous bosom, staring feverishly at those male hands as they took her measure and made their notes, and as I looked down it hit me! This was where the real music was. This was why all the women down there danced the way they did, why they let themselves be held around the waist and promenaded beneath the trees and why they placed their hands on their partners' necks. They did it for the old women to see, these women who no longer had anyone to touch, who would never again be embraced that way, which was why the old women's eyes sparkled as they did, why they glowed with longing and envy and resentment; and I saw that there were walls not just dividing symphonic music from brass-band music, but people from people as well, walls far more real than the one I was sitting on, gazing down and seeing everything at once, so mesmerized it's a wonder I didn't go plunging off. And the little man tugged at me again and urged me to intervene, because the dancers below were shaking their fists and shouting at the orchestra, "To hell with your A major!"

And then I turned and saw that some members of the symphony audience were climbing up all three ladders through the aviary, and then the dancers in the brewery courtyard started bringing up ladders and leaning them up against the wall and pushing their way up, and it was like those pictures you see of castles under siege, they were glaring at each other as though some unseen conductor were directing them, and now they were standing on top of the wall, and I saw them close in on each other, their eyes flaming with hatred, and they began swinging at each other, and several of them stumbled and plunged down off the wall, but I was already somewhere else, I could no longer acknowledge the truth of either side with my fists so I tore off a small branch and began conducting both orchestras, and Mr. Polata's band began to play *With Lion's Strength the Falcon Soars*, and the waitresses quickly cleared the beer off the tables, and the shadow of a falling body would flit past, and they were all so united by passion that more of them climbed up the ladders, and by now the top of the wall was jammed not just with sandstone statues but with brawlers as well, some of them so beside themselves with rage they began wrestling with the statues, and the Prague Municipal Symphony Orchestra stopped playing and those musicians ran under the branches of the ancient trees and Mr. Polata's band stopped playing as well and those musicians crowded round at the foot of the wall, some of them climbing up the ladders, and on the other side of the wall, the symphony musicians did the same, bringing their instruments with them, so that now there were instruments as well as people on the wall, and the musicians began to fight, their shiny instruments flashing back and forth, tearing down branches, and it was strange to see trumpets and euphoniums going at each other, and clarinets fencing with clarinets, and every once in a while a body would plummet off the wall, but that didn't stop admirers of Mr. Polata's music from gathering down below, and on their side of the wall, fans of the Prague Municipal Symphony Orchestra did the same, all shaking their fists at one another and shouting while they made room for Mr. Polata himself to climb up the ladder on one side and Mr. Smetáček on the other, so they, too, could have a go at each other. But then, amid wailing sirens, a milk-white police car swerved into the brewery courtyard and another nosed through the gates of the Waldstein Gardens, as if they had given each other a signal, or had taken their directions from my baton, but by then the melée on top of the wall was so intense that someone grabbed me and shoved me, but I managed to hang on to his coat, and it was a fan of Mr. Polata's music, and he fell down into the Waldstein Gardens, and at the same time I flew headfirst, arms spread wide, down into Mr. Polata's orchestra and crashed into the drum set, then toppled over into the slippery pool of saliva the trombonist had blown out of his instrument.... The cops leaped out of their squad cars, and, as if on command, the old ladies on the second and third floors flung open all the windows, and reflections from the glass flitted across the sky, across the walls and the upturned faces, and in that strange, pallid light I saw everything and heard everything, and I was in harmony with everything and accepted everything and the old ladies were shouting over each other, flailing their bony arms and yelling, "Down with big-breasted women! Lock them up! Chop off their hands! Rip out their tongues! Set the gelders and castrators on them!" And forever after I was a rotten ticket taker and a rotten organizer because, after everything I'd seen and heard today and yesterday, I had kicked my way through a drum and come out somewhere on the other side, because I saw everything as if it were wrapped in a single enormous bundle. Only my idiot brother-in-law was sitting backwards on his chair, wagging his finger and pointing at people and saying: "I'd give that one a passport, but not this one; I'd let this one travel abroad, but not that one." And the brawl on the wall crescendoed, and clusters of brawlers came tumbling down, and they were so wedged in together that they fought without knowing why anymore, and when the lamps turned out, they no longer knew who they were fighting with. There were only bodies falling in the dark and there was the sound of wailing ... but I was in harmony with everything and I was saved, too, but lost in a way as well ... but I think this will probably be my salvation....

Beautiful Poldi

Whatever became of that blind man who sold newspapers outside Masaryk Station? Where did he go? He'd stand there peddling his wares, and when a cold wind blew he'd rifle through his papers like a rotary press spilling out pages while pedestrians leaning into the blast would pass him by, averting their eyes from the sight of the blind man battling the wind for possession of his wares, the pages flipping over like leaves on a daily calendar. Whatever became of that blind man? Where did he go?

And what about that cripple on Wenceslas Square? Whatever became of him? He'd sell his mechanical toys on the sidewalk outside Čekans, winding up a little metallic beetle, releasing it into the air, and catching it again in his outstretched arms. Sometimes, when he'd have to chase the toy under the linden trees lining the square, he looked as though he were wading in cobblestones up to his waist, since both his legs had been amputated at the hip, leaving him nothing to fasten artificial limbs to. Where did that cripple go? Whatever became of him?

And what about the woman whose feet were amputated above the ankles? Whatever became of her? She'd walk around Prague as if on her knees and she wore men's galoshes backwards. After a fresh snowfall, I'd see her approaching from St. Havel's though trackless snow, and from her footprints, it looked as if she'd been walking beside me, though she was heading in the opposite direction. Wherever did that woman go?

Often these days I see a large star and think it must be the Evening Star, but it's a tongue of flame from a welder's torch, a wistful little blue flame, the Holy Spirit descending and flaring red when it touches iron. I open a window of the factory hall and watch the fellow on top of a heap of wartime scrap, holding the bright star tightly between his fingers as he pulls the rubber hoses behind him, the burning jet spewing Christmas-tree sparklers.

At the Poldi steelworks, hopeless people hold their muddied hopes aloft. Life, strangely enough, is constantly being reinvented, and loved, even though a tinfoil brain will bring forth crumpled images, and a trampled torso will ooze misery. And yet, it is still a beautiful thing when a man abandons his three square meals a day and his adding machine and his family and goes off to follow a beautiful star. Life is still magnificent as long as one maintains the illusion that an entire world can be conjured from a tiny patch of earth. When a volunteer laborer has a hundred days left in his stint, he buys a yellow folding ruler and snips off a centimeter a day. When the final piece slips from his fingers, he passes through the neck of a bottle on his way to somewhere else, to encounter another adventure.

But beautiful Poldi is also a volunteer laborer's scream that tears to shreds all the signs and slogans, three crowns fifty per hundred grams, because you return to the depths of your brain to study the bill to see what you've bought and why you've paid so much, because the man who turns his hand to fruitful labor is saved forever. Life is fidelity to the beauty exploding all around us, even, at times, at the cost of our own lives. The newspapers, meanwhile, publish glowing accounts of the volunteer laborer who comes home from work and dances the Cossack Dance while sending mental telegrams of gratitude to the authorities, whereas in reality he coughs up black bile and collapses into his bed. Or a thirsty drop of molten steel swims through a roller's eye, his wife's image vanishes, and he tries, with ludicrous little steps, to dance away from his misfortune. Progress dines at times on roasted youth; a silver ambulance carries off someone with his feet against the glass doors; a crushed arm longs to return to the shape it once had; and what hurts most about a severed leg is the toe that has vanished with it.

The white-gowned doctor washes his hands. "Are you a believer, young lady?" he asks.

"Yes, but doctor ..."

"Well, then, young lady, you must believe. Concentrate, pray, believe with all your might, because my science is no longer of any use."

He washes his hands and avoids her eye, for why get upset? Does the doctor know that at this very moment, or an hour from now, certainly by this evening at the latest, a trap somewhere will snap shut and an ambulance will arrive to gather the prey? There will always be a trusting newbie who fails to get a proper grip on the red-hot wire with his pliers, or the tongs fly apart and kick him, or he bungles the extrusion of hot wire and sixteen meters of fiery filament spins into the air and the rollers leap out of the way or take shelter under the rolling bench, but sometimes a loop of it touches the newbie's neck and forces him to dance a dance for his buddies in the finishing room, his dance a variation on the statuary of Laocoön and his sons, in which minimal contact elicits maximum pain, and if the thirsty filament doesn't sear his jaw, it will char his cheek bones; if it doesn't burn through his clavicle, it will scorch the fingers that try to remove this cup from his lips and in the end, the newbie's head drops, his lips are fused together in an eternally malodorous kiss, and through the seared collarbone the spirit unlocks its torture chamber and beautiful Poldi grows fatter. Young men in the fiery furnace. And yet when the wounds heal and they go back to work, these volunteer laborers are bettering everything on life.

"Hey, Annie, if I had a guy like that at home? I'd grease the stairs, kick his butt, and send him flying, I swear by the blessed Virgin, I would."

"So the Captain says, 'Everyone get out of the boat and push!'"

"Who's he telling that to? Who's he talking to? Did anyone on this bus ask him? No one. Aha! Hector's licking his ice-cream bar. But we're doing him wrong. He's not stupid, he's just a little thick."

"So what? Either you get run over in Prague, or here."

"See that? Hear that? He's talking to himself. He's got his wires crossed. When it comes to thinking, he's walking on his hands."

"Miss, hold that pose. It's as if you were alive."

"My grandmother? She could still piss without her glasses on right into her nineties."

"Driver, step on it, or they'll declare you missing in action. I want to get back in time to go to the movies tomorrow."

"Ooo, careful, here comes a crossroads! Better get a notarized certificate that nothing's coming the other way!"

"If the driver went for cherries, he'd come back with plums."

"I had chicken soup at Hunecks, but there were teeth marks in the thigh from the previous customer. The goddamned chicken probably played soccer all her life for the local eleven and then died of old age."

"I'm going to sit beside you." "Please don't, I'm not insured."

"When the old gal wouldn't fit in the coffin, we broke her legs."

"It's all a matter of contingencies. If elephant grass started growing ten meters high, we'd have the dinosaurs back in three days."

"For God's sake, Blazka, get your ass out of my face!"

"Ever since their place got burgled, they've been fond of each other."

"But I want to know who's guilty! Just don't blame it on the Bible."

"It was enemas that brought me and my wife together. We have some splendid secrets."

"Today, when they tell me to jump in the lake, I jump in the water."

"Of course she's not a woman! She's an out-and-out cow."

"In the name of decency, comrades, would you please speak politely on this bus?"

"František, you're completely out to lunch! Wine has to mature in the barrel. It will never ripen in bottles."

"Okay, say you cut off a girl's pigtail as a prank. That's not an insult to her dignity, it's a crime. It's an invasion of her personal space."

"Merciful heavens, I wish you actuaries would actually finish at least one game of *mariáš.*"

"Poldi Recreation Centre! Koněv Spa! Everyone off the bus!"

Among other things, beautiful Poldi is tar pits and slag heaps and barracks and dormitories. Barbed wire separates the steel works from fields of undulating grain and vegetable gardens. The smell of stale urine wafts through the open windows of the dormitory, where sleepers sleep in layers on makeshift bunks, exactly as they'd fallen asleep after their night shifts, their forearms exposed to receive injections of light. Hirsute men with broken spines and crippled hands play cards, lending a frenzied authority to their loud banter. It's as though the entire camp were on the alert, waiting for something fundamental to happen: a knock on the door, the sound of a voice, something that would instantly render everyone good and beautiful. From outside comes the strident clamor of slogans over a loudspeaker and an accordion optimistically paints cheap color prints. And yet there is not a single flower on the laborers' table, not one little bouquet for the world to lean on.

From where I'm standing in the dormitory doorway, the corridor is so long I can barely see to the door at the other end. When I've walked the length of it and turned around, the doorway I've come from is no bigger than a tiny window. A barracks like this is a rattrap sprung shut by a perspective constantly narrowing at either end. The old attendant who brought me here grows smaller and smaller as he walks down the corridor, until he's tiny: a figurine standing in that apparently miniature window at the end of the hall. When I opened the door to the dormitory, the air was alive with rings and golden squares, as though someone had been playing carelessly with shrapnel. The only unbroken things in the room were two mustard jars. The padlocks on the lockers were as twisted as arthritic fingers. Then, a volunteer laborer came up to me and said his name was Jarda Jezule, a furrier. In one hand he held a small suitcase, and in the other the Collected Works of Karl Marx. Beside him was a broken stove with the stovepipe sticking out of the wall like a huge piece of excrement oozing from a music-hall giant. Jarda Jezule sat down on an upper bunk, and I lay on the bed beneath. He took off a boot and a sock, and his feet were tiny, red from scarlet fever, withered and wrinkled like the soles of a Chinese girl's foot or the inside of a bulldog's mouth. He massaged his toes to get the blood moving again, then he stuffed newspapers in the toes of his boots and as he did so, he dangled his feet in my face. I lay on the bunk below as if in a river where the furrier was dipping his feet. Meanwhile, the camp echoed with voices calling out to each other. The aroma of the washroom and the toilets seeped through the wall. The languid sounds of a music box drifted in from a playground, and through the window you could see, across the way, another dormitory, just as big, the buildings laid out like a military hospital.

Beautiful Poldi, however, is also the path that leads away from the dormitories, past a black pond where an electric pump spews out a stream of water. In the pond, a gypsy woman stands on a stone next to a rusty stove and a half-submerged bicycle, washing her ragged clothes. Jarda Jezule and I walk this way to the Black Horse to play the piano and drink rum. The Collected Works are under the bed, but we're in no state to read. After all, during a single shift at the blast furnace we drank twenty beers and peed scarcely a cupful. With the last of our money, we shoot for plastic roses at the shooting gallery. Then we walk back. The female convicts are already in their dorms, housed in barracks separated from ours by a board fence topped with barbed wire. Only today I noticed, through a knothole in the fence, that these female prisoners live in a tidy place with clean tablecloths and bouquets of meadow flowers, while we who are free live in a pigsty. One of the prisoners is a stunning beauty who threw her mother down a well, and when the mother clawed her way back up to the light, that gorgeous young woman split her head open with an axe. Two of the volunteer laborers tried to reach the murderess by climbing over the fence, but the guards caught them just as they were trying to touch her, and they got slapped around and were given three months each in jail. At the rolling mill I handed her a flower. It was as though the murder and the punishment had purified her, and today she could be leading a proper life, with tablecloths, flowers, and kind words. When she took a bath each evening, every knothole in the fence was occupied by a laborer's eye. She was covered in soft, fine hair, a light golden down, as if her entire body were wrapped in a halo. When she soaped herself, she would pause to daydream and stand in odd poses. We tried in vain to make telescopes of our eyes, while the stronger men pushed the weaker ones away from the knotholes. I could see that she knew every eye in every knothole and that she'd come to expect them and that she bathed naked for the sake for those longing male gazes, which, for her, took the place of a stroll along the boulevard in the evening. But what devastated the laborers most of all was not her naked body, but the shadow play she put on in the dormitory by her bed. She would hang a sheet in the window and position a lightbulb to cast the shadow of her lascivious movement against the sheet. It was like watching a movie. We'd all jump up and down on the other side of the fence, crawl up to the barbed wire, fall back down again, pick ourselves up, but as soon as we fixed our eyes to the knot holes again and saw the shadow play, we were climbing up the fence again, trying to get over it and into that bird cage, because that beautiful, naked prisoner would reach out to us with her shadowy arms and there was so much desire in her movements that each man thought she was reaching out just for him, to each of us, one by one. Then, when she reckoned she'd toyed with us enough, she'd put on a sweatsuit, take down the sheet, make her bed, and lie down on her bunk like the others, light a cigarette, put her arms behind her damp head, and read a cheap romance novel. We'd go back to our barracks, leaving behind the still-illuminated women's dorm with its female prisoners, who put bouquets of cornflowers and wild poppies on every table. But at a barred washroom window, a half-mad female prisoner rested her head on the windowsill, listening to the sounds of "The Harlequin's Millions" coming from the music box in the shooting gallery. A teardrop glittered like a diamond in the ring of her eye. When they're at the bottom, people fill their eyes with beautiful things. The world is full of art, it's just a matter of knowing how to look around you and then surrendering to inexhaustible whisperings, to small details, to longing and desire.

But beautiful Poldi is also the moment when a grinder suddenly tears off his safety glasses, flees his work, and goes outside as far away as he can; he looks into the sky, then at the mountain of rusting scrap metal, at the birds who come to drink from the boiling pools by mistake; he watches as a tiny scalded body hops into the rusty pipes and thinks how everything has its own torture chamber, but also its own paradise. And the grinder goes back to his post, dons his safety goggles, presses the button, and starts working again, feeding the yard engine shuttling back and forth to the furnaces. Everyone is possessed, at times, with the desire to rebel. Man has refused to live in a primitive state of nature, which is why angels drive ambulances and gather up other angels who have been broken in half.

I love going to the works canteen beside the sleeping warehouse, where the slabs and billets and blooms are stacked in neat layers like oaken logs. Outside, I look at the sky, where a woman's head suddenly appears, as large as the night sky itself, a head of curly hair singed by stars, her countenance filled with never-before-perceived detail. Steel with an admixture of wolfram and cobalt will, when sliced into, show colors like those of an Asiatic butterfly's wings. Someone pumps sentences into my brain, long-forgotten images from childhood; meaningless objects and conversations peel layers from my heart. I am again a river faun, paralyzed by longing for a river nymph. I walk through wolframic space, my mouth and nose threaded with wire, and whenever I deviate from my course, I feel a sharp pain in my jaws.

I approach the electrolytic furnace, a tablet of blue glass before my eyes, and the molten metal gurgles violently. This is the magnificent work of magnificent people. The roar of the blast furnaces echoes through the hall like a symphony orchestra, and a single glance carries me through the furnace's hearth, back to that staircase where you and I carried a lamp to the pawn shop, when my hand first touched yours; melodic rollers milled my heart, dusty mannequins suddenly froze, sharp-eyed and conventional; your rocking-chair walk galvanized my brain and the lightning bolt of my feeling electrified your hair. After that, for the sake of love, one could plunge into the molten metal: make steel with an admixture of myself and your image within me, an image that calls to mind a small, childlike face flushed with gentle, silly laughter, because a Jewish girl spat out razor blades and I slashed my wrists. Beautiful blueberry nights fill my liver with morning and the nozzle of my heart spews forth an amalgam of blood. The sun rides the elevator up from the darkness, and the silken, waving wheat sways like a woman's raw cotton skirt. The wheels of the pit-head elevator turn backward, and columns of cherry-tree trunks girdled with white lime reveal the hidden location of military burial grounds. Watchmen guard the female convicts in their wire enclosure, and swallows deliver the message of violins in their beaks. The women prisoners form lines, and I look for my beauty, but she's not there yet. Some of the girls comb their hair like high-toned ladies. They roll up the sleeves and legs of their cotton blouses and trousers like millionaire heiresses sunning themselves on the beaches of Miami. The world is sustained by these girlish shapes, by lipstick, toothbrushes, face cream, and by male eyes. They are bandages and sticky plaster that will stay in place for ten, fifteen, twenty years at a stretch. Even a lifetime. A siskin sings in a cage at the entrance to the women's camp, its eyes put out to make it sing more melodically. Sweetness fills my chest: I smell nail polish, vats of chocolate, and slaughterhouse stun guns. I think of empty cigarette cases, miniature lightbulbs, graveyard candle chimneys, a gold-leaf press, crowns of thorns, and organtine. Lilies of the Valley flow from my eyes. Beautiful Poldi, an impression in copper, tiny head on a fragrant medallion, the aroma of hair singed by stars, I will garland you with the most beautiful things I have ever seen, I will speak with you through dead objects, I will address you when enamel jugs fall from the sky, when the mad moon mirrors the reflections of your reflection. The air itself is anointed with you. I need only dial the number, and an amethyst telephone will be answered at the other end, and from your mouth, air will flow transmitted by tiny electromagnetic waves, frozen words, constellations, human tissue, laboratory ovens, bridges going nowhere, and a vibrator. Oh, if only I could lend you my eyes! It is so marvelous to be in love, to carry one's own tiny electric motor around with one. Why, even the touch of a razor can last for twenty years and more. There is always more of me when I think of you, Poldi. As if through you, I've conquered a diamond universe.

I recline on my bunk, but first I use a match to immolate the bedbugs in the cracks. The sun knits a gem-studded stocking. I write your name in chalk on the boards of the bunk above me, where Jarda Jezule twists and turns angrily in his sheets and bits of straw from his mattress float into my eyes. Someone has driven a knife into the broken cupboard. Jarda Jezule sits up and lets his small red foot dangle down; the toes like a set of teeth.

"Hey, Jezule," I say, "where do you keep your reading matter – those Collected Works?"

"What Collected Works?"

"The ones you brought with you," I say, and I draw Poldi's head on the board, her hair singed by a star.

"Would you lay off!" Jarda replies, poking his head down. "I've lost five kilos. What about these bed bugs? What about that shithouse right next door?"

"There were poets in concentration camps, too," I say, and carry on with my drawing. "Jezule, a little romanticism never ..."

"But this isn't a concentration camp!" Jarda shouts, the blood rushing to his face.

"That's right," I say. "It's not, but nothing lasts forever. There's not an ounce of the romantic in you, Jezule, not a single ounce."

Jarda, volunteer laborer and former furrier, grasps the side of the bunk, leaning down, his face spouting hostility, a cathedral gargoyle. He jumps down, his red feet slapping the floor hard, then he hobbles over and brandishes his finger in my face like a knife, holding my eyes in check for a whole minute, as though he wanted to tell me something terribly important. Then he waves his hand, dismissing the terribly important thing and me along with it. He spits, then begins stuffing newspaper into the toes of his boots.

"Hey, Kafka," he says calmly, "Does that lice ointment help? Does it help?"

"It helps," I say. "It helps."

"So Kafka, my buddy, go to bed. You're just off the night-shift, get some sleep," Jarda Jezule says, picking up his boot and peering into it with scientific curiosity. As I'm drifting off I can hear him rummaging under the bed and dusting some books off on his knee.

And again, morning after morning, I arise and have no time to think about myself or to wonder: Am I happy? Am I unhappy? I am aware, before it happens, of that first mechanical motion of my hand, reaching for the alarm clock, I grope sleepily between its legs to stop the clanging of its nickel-plated testicles. Then, with the same groping motion, I fumble for the light switch on the wall and undertake the first shy self-examination of a man prematurely woken up, his hair in disarray, smelly, someone sitting up on his bed one more time, holding an alarm clock. Each morning I turn on the radio, tune in to Berlin and listen.... There's dead air at first but then, a few minutes before four a.m., "The Internationale" comes on, sung by a choir with an orchestra, then a sweet, familiar voice says: "Good morning, comrades! Moscow calling," then thirty seconds of silence, followed by the sudden morning sounds of a busy Moscow street near the Kremlin, whistles, honking horns, sirens, and the bells of the Kremlin begin to peal ... one, two, three, four, five, six times, then the pleasant voice comes on again: "Comrades, this is Moscow calling! Good morning, it's six o'clock," then "The Internationale" again, rendered by the choir and orchestra, which means it's four a.m. here, which means I have three more minutes, making it worthwhile to slip back into bed and watch the second hand tick slowly forward, around once, twice, and again. Sometimes I even doze off for those three minutes, but then I must arise and surrender to the automatism, terrible, yet precise, especially in the morning, when there's no choice but to come to life, get dressed quickly, brush the teeth of the doppelgänger in the mirror, and wonder why I shave every other day and wash and eat several times a day, and go around with a seating plan in my brain. Why worry constantly about missing out on something? You must be brave, I console myself, you must, you must, you must! I repeat the mantra every hour, but in the morning, I say it every minute, the better to brush aside nagging thoughts. I leave the house and it starts to rain, a thin drizzle shrouding the countryside and my garden, and I feel how much I need the rain. I feel the dark water pushing through to the roots, washing away the limestone dust. I feel my pores smacking their lips, I become a Golden Russet, a Winesap, a Topaz, a Melba Red and I begin to wonder what else I might need to be any happier. I crave potash, phosphorus, nitrogen. I open my eyes, and my automatic pilot has long since planted me in a seat on the bus, and I become aware of how I'm being sucked out by perspective, out into the streets that converge at a point in the distance, becoming so narrow a bicycle could scarcely squeeze through; and yet, when we reach that point, two buses can pass abreast and a new perspective mendaciously offers the prospect of miniature objects on the horizon. Vehicles approaching from a distance are as alike as two points of a colon, then growing until the headlights sweep by, and I see it's another bus just like ours. For an instant, we mirror each other, and moments later I see a pair of red taillights grow smaller, until they vanish prematurely. I look around and I'm not alone. Some of the workers are asleep, still dreaming, or lost in thought. The small emerald light on the driver's dashboard is beautiful and as large as any visible star. The driver keeps his eyes simultaneously on the road ahead, on both sides, and in the side and rearview mirrors, while monitoring the engine, accelerating or decelerating, working the clutch and the brake with his feet, controlling the steering wheel with his hands. In Vokovice, as he does every morning, he leans out and looks up at the same window and says, "She's up!" If the window is dark, he honks the horn, stops the bus, and honks again, until a light goes on, then the bus continues contentedly on its way. I imagine that inside that window there's a bed belonging to a post-office clerk, who has an arrangement with the bus driver, and I see her, sitting on the edge of her straw mattress, ready to put on her stockings, wondering if it's worth getting up, and then, when she sees the tousle-haired girl in the mirror, she asks: why go on living? But the bus is already driving on down the road, past Ruzyně airport, its runway illuminated in anticipation of an arrival, lined with ruby lights that converge at the far end of the landing strip where anyone standing would see our bus passing by that point. . . . The aircraft casts a cone of light on the runway, approaches the earth, grows smaller as it touches down, as tiny now as a child's elastic-powered model plane, the wings swinging around, the navigation lights reversing, and once again it grows larger as it approaches the terminal, though it is still the same size. . . . I close my eyes and see that everything is quite different from how it appears, from what it is. . . . Everything exists in the elasticity of perspective, and life itself is illusion, deformation, perspective. . . . I open my eyes, and we've arrived at the steelworks. The volunteer laborers rouse each other: Get up, they've brought you a load of coke. And like the others, I shuffle listlessly through the factory gate, show my I.D., and walk to the showers and the changing room. I see the yard engine chugging around the bend pulling a 4500-kilo load of red-hot steel slabs still glowing pink. Like young girls off to their first dance, the ingots seem able to conceal their true essence and appear instead to be made of crepe paper pumped full of warm air, prevented by a mere string from soaring into the air like balloons, airy and graceful and unreal. The locomotive spews clouds of steam, and almost, it seems, with its last ounce of strength, it drags its payload in pink past me, so close it singes my hair and clothes, and I am left in no doubt that these are tons and tons of steel, obelisks so long and so wide, and for a moment I see them more or less as they are, but then they immediately diminish and as I move away I accelerate their diminishment, while altering nothing in the reality of the yard engine and its slabs of steel.... I quickly doff my streetclothes, and following my daily routine, I pull on a tank-top, then a shirt, then boxer shorts, then sweat pants, then trousers, then I put on my boots, then a cat-skin vest, then my overall pants and top, then an apron and gloves, and finish it off with a helmet, and finally, like the other workers, I walk quickly out into the night. The morning star – huge, but no bigger than the emerald light on the bus driver's dashboard – glitters in the firmament, marking the beginning of all morning shifts and at the same time, the end of every night shift. I turn around and on the distant hillside, I can see the yard engine laboring up the slope with its 4500 kilos of pink ingots; the train is small and different now and yet the same one that not long ago singed my clothes and hair. Now it's climbing Koněv and up there on the hillside it is tiny, no bigger than a child's toy train on a string.... Everything exists in the elasticity of perspective.

Translator's afterword

"If you knew how much I love the Poldi steel mill, you'd be jealous. It was there that I saw everything, and from the moment I saw her, I became a seer."
　　　　　－Bohumil Hrabal, from *Be Kind Enough to Pull
　　　　　Down the Blinds: A Selection of Love Letters*

Hrabal's fascination with an industry he describes as "the magnificent work of magnificent people" has roots in the history of the region. Originally, the Kladno steel works, about forty kilometers northeast of Prague, consisted of two separate companies. The first, the Vojtěšska Iron Works, was founded in the 1850s when Bohemia was still part of the Austro-Hungarian empire. By the end of that century, it had become the largest of its kind in the monarchy, smelting ore and scrap metal into tens of thousands of tons of iron and steel each year to supply the needs of the industrial revolution.

In 1889, a second company, the Poldi Steel Works, was established nearby to produce high-quality steel. The founder, Karl Wittgenstein (who was also the father of the philosopher Ludwig Wittgenstein) named it after his wife, Leopoldina, known to family and friends as Poldi. He registered a cameo profile of her, with a star poised above her head, as the company trademark that would later inspire Hrabal to personify the steelworks as a woman in "Beautiful Poldi."

After 1948, when the Communists, with Soviet backing, usurped power in Czechoslovakia, the two companies were merged into a single nationalized enterprise. The Vojtěšska steel mill – where Hrabal worked as a "volunteer" from 1949 to 1954 – was renamed "Koněv" after the Red Army field marshal who had liberated large parts of Eastern Europe from Nazi occupation. For commercial reasons, the Communists left the Poldi name and trademark intact, and the entire area eventually came to be known as simply Poldi Kladno. That company, with its logo, is still in operation today. The Koněv works were shut down and abandoned in 1975.

Today, against the backdrop of Poldi's new glass-and-steel factory halls, smokestacks, and electrical plants, all that remains of Hrabal's Koněv is a forlorn and ghostly tract of weeds, rubble, corroded gas pipelines, rusting rail spurs, crumbling lime kilns, blackened coke-storage facilities, and derelict buildings. The proud blast furnaces that were once the heart of the industry are gone, having been dismantled and recycled to become raw material for the new, post-communist era. Walking through the silent ruins is like visiting an ancient archaeological site that mere decades ago teemed with a bizarre and anomalous life in the shadow of Stalinism. It is this life that Hrabal chronicles in this book.

The "volunteer" laborers in Hrabal's stories – judges and lawyers, poets and philosophy professors, policemen, army officers, tradesmen, and small businessmen – were all uprooted from their former lives by the Communist regime as part of a program called "Putting 77,000 to Work," during which tens of thousands were plucked from their jobs and sent to mines, factories, and collective farms to perform unfamiliar work in harsh and dangerous conditions, alongside regular workers, party hacks, criminals, and political prisoners. This was how the former railway dispatcher, insurance agent, lawyer, traveling salesman, and aspiring writer Bohumil Hrabal, found himself working in the Kladno steel mills.

Hrabal accepted his fate with an open mind, and it marked a turning point in his creative life. For well over a decade, under the influence of the Surrealists and other writers, he had been experimenting with different literary forms – poetry, brief impressionistic prose "études," dream chronicles, automatic writing – all the time groping for a way of doing justice to the unprecedented strangeness of life in a newly "revolutionary" society. Eventually, this led to a creative crisis, of sorts:

> I had begun building my house from the roof on down … always emphasizing the façade and the decorative touches.... I had borrowed a little from Rimbaud, a little from Baudelaire, a little from Éluard, and again from Céline. I used artificial clusters of words as though they were natural linguistic signs, and so I invented more and more impossible metaphors – until Kladno, in the steelworks, where my whole, pseudo-artistic, second-hand world collapsed, and for an entire year I merely looked around me and saw and heard fundamental things and fundamental words. It was some time before I realized that I had to start again from the ground up, give up trying to escape and begin to write as if I were writing for

the newspapers, reporting on people and their conversations, their work, and in general, their lives.

The stories in this collection represent the early results of Hrabal's discovery of what he came to call "total realism," the realization that the ordinary events of everyday life can be as magical as surrealism, and that straightforward accounts of people at work and in conversation can reveal more about who they are and the world they live in than attempts to portray their inner lives. Hrabal's characters pass the time in conversation, with themselves and with each other, from idle banter about women, history, or the relative merits of Czech poets – like the communist icon Vitězslav Nezval or the patriotic lyricist Jaroslav Vrchlický – to current affairs and personal stories that lay bare the very essence of their lives.

Some are outliers, like the Milkman in "Strange People," a true volunteer who discovers that his ideals clash with the demands of those in power, and that his appeals to highly placed Communist officials, like Antonín "Tonda" Zápotocký, would fall on deaf ears. Others are merely hoping to survive the huge disruption to their lives with a shred of dignity. Still others achieve a kind of inner peace, a new and deeper understanding of themselves, as they come to terms with the harsh reality they have been forced to undergo.

Like the times they chronicle, Hrabal's stories can sometimes be disturbingly raw, and elements of his early surrealistic poetics still cling to them, in particular in the two stories that bookend the collection, "Mr. Kafka," and "Beautiful Poldi," both of which Hrabal originally wrote, in 1950, as "epic" poems and then later reworked as prose.

Chronologically, the stories straddle a period from roughly

the closing years of World War II, when the narrator of "Breaking Through the Drum" was just embarking on his career as an usher, through the postwar, pre-communist period ("Mr. Kafka"), to 1962, when de-Stalinization was in full swing and the most grandiose statue to Stalin in the world – unveiled in 1955 two years after Stalin's death, even as the Generalissimo's cult was about to be radically dismantled in places like Poland and Hungary – was destroyed. That event serves Hrabal as a backdrop for the two parallel narratives in "A Betrayal of Mirrors": the story of the hapless stonemason who reluctantly takes part in the restoration of cultural monuments that have been allowed to go derelict, and of the beleaguered artist Mr. Valerián, who against his better judgment takes part in a competition to revive public interest in Alois Jirásek and his retelling of old Czech legends that, under Stalinism, were condemned as expressions of "bourgeois nationalism."

Apart from appearances in small magazines in the late 1950s, Hrabal published nothing officially until 1963, when his first book of stories, *Pearls on the Bottom*, appeared. The present collection, under the title *Want-ad for a House I no Longer Wish to Live in*, came out in 1965 and was his fourth book. Like all literature at the time, it was subject to censorship, which is why I have based my translations on the restored versions of these stories that appeared in the post-1989 edition of Hrabal's *Collected Writings*.

This is the second book of Hrabal's I have translated (the first was *I Served the King of England*), but *Mr. Kafka* was by far the more challenging task, and I was fortunate to find people willing to help me understand the technical and linguistic obscurities in Hrabal's text. Still, some passages baffled even the experts, leaving me to take my best guess at Hrabal's meaning. Of course I accept full responsibility for any errors.

My thanks to Monika Horsáková and Josef Chrobák, both of whom teach at the Silesian University in Opava; and to Tomáš Voldráb, a curator at the Mayrau mining museum near Kladno, who helped me understand the processes involved in turning ore and scrap metal into steel. A special thanks to my old friend Zbýšek Sion, one of Hrabal's greatest fans. Zbýšek introduced me to the person whose help and advice has been the most invaluable of all – Tomáš Mazal, a friend of Hrabal's, and the author of several helpful books about him and his life and times.

At New Directions, my thanks to Declan Spring for the assignment, for his patience and his many helpful editing suggestions; and to Dan Stiles, the cover designer, for capturing the spirit of the book in a single vivid image.

And last, but certainly foremost, to my wife, Patricia, for her unfailing support and her eagle eye, from first draft to final proofs.

I'd like to dedicate this translation to the memory of Věra Sýkorová, with whom I taught English at the secondary school Na Zatlance in Prague in the early 1970s. Věra was the wife of the poet and musician Karel Maryška, a close friend of Hrabal's, and as I knew her, she would have been one of the people Hrabal had in mind when, in his introduction to this book, he praised those heroes who did not succumb to the "semantic confusion" of their times.

PAUL WILSON, AUGUST 2015